DOTTY

and the Calendar House Key

Emma Warner-Reed

First published by Calendar House Press 2016

Cover design by Emma Warner-Reed

Designed and Typeset by Emma Warner-Reed

The DOTTY Series Vol. 1 – DOTTY and the Calendar
House Key

Summary:

Following the death of her parents in a tragic firework
accident, nine and a half year old Welsh girl, Dotty Parsons, is
sent to live with her Great Uncle Winchester at The Calendar
House - a vast old country house in deepest, darkest Yorkshire.

Once there, Dotty is disturbed by noises coming from the
chimneys and soon suspects everything is not as it seems. The
cook tells her the noises are just jackdaws nesting. But in
December - surely that can't be right, can it?

ISBN:978-0-9955662-1-7

For Florence.

CONTENTS

Contents

ACKNOWLEDGMENTS

My sincerest thanks go as always to my husband, Jonathan, and to my beautiful little family, the latest addition to which this book is dedicated.

I would also like to thank my friends for their kind input and advice, and all of those close friends and family who have supported me in buying advance copies of the book. I hope the read is worth the wait!

But by far my biggest thank you must go to Alex Vere, to whom I owe an eternal debt of gratitude. Not only has she been my inspiration in writing this book, she has also been a tireless supporter of my cause, my editor, proof-reader, reviewer, designer, tea maker, general emotional crutch and guru of all things technical to do with the book and its publication. I simply cannot thank you enough, my friend.

Prologue

Never Play with Fireworks

Dotty Parsons was sad. Immeasurably sad. Not least because ever since the accident nobody called her Dotty any more. Despite all her best protestations the firemen, the hospital staff, the social workers, the community police officer, in fact *all* the adults insisted on calling her by her full name: Dorothea. Apart from the simple fact that the name Dorothea didn't suit her (far too grown up a name for a nine and a half year old), Dotty's mum and dad had never once in her whole nine and a half years called her that. The only thing that had ever come close was when she had been exceptionally bad, in which case she was "DOROTHEA MADELAAAAINE!" But never, not *ever*, was she plain Dorothea. Dotty longed more than anything to be Dotty again.

Never Play with Fireworks

It had all happened on a Tuesday. There was nothing out of the ordinary about this particular drizzly November evening in suburban Cardiff: nothing that singled it out for disaster, except that it was bonfire night and Dotty's mum and dad had agreed, after much pleading from Dotty, to hold a firework party in their tiny back garden.

The party was the cause of great excitement for both Dotty and her best friend and classmate Sylv (short for Sylvia – a name her friend hated in its full form almost as much as Dotty hated her own). As a consequence, the afternoon at St Aidan's primary school had dragged on for what seemed like an eternity. With growing impatience they eagerly awaited the school bell and the evening's entertainment that was to follow.

Monsieur Evans' weekly French lesson, followed by a very damp and drizzly double PE with the ample Mrs Thwistletot (the most unlikely gym teacher the girls thought it possible to find) were both equally tortuous. But finally the bell went and the girls raced out of school, Sylv still wearing her netball banner, 'GK' emblazoned in forest green on front and back. Mrs Thwistletot waddled after them, waving coats and remonstrating breathily in her thick Welsh accent:

"Now then girls, slow down! You've forgotten your jackets." The girls giggled. "And mind you look both ways as you cross the road."

"Come on Dotty I'll race you home," laughed Sylv, pulling on her anorak haphazardly as she ran.

Dotty's house was on Wyvern Road, only two blocks and a single road crossing away from school. Sylv lived in the neighbouring semi. The fact that the girls had only been allowed to make the journey home together unsupervised since the beginning of the school year, and that there was still an element of novelty to it, only added to their excitement as they made their way back to Dotty's. In fact such was their enthusiasm that they would have missed their daily pit stop for sherbet refreshers at Eddie Raman's corner shop, perched rather conveniently at the end of Dotty's street, were it not for Eddie's son, Joe, calling out to them as they passed the ever-open shop door.

"Hiya, girls! You not buying today?"

Little Joe Raman was only seven and a half but already an experienced salesman. Coming to an abrupt halt, the girls found him in his usual spot behind the counter of the cramped and gloomy newsagents, wearing a disproportionately shocked expression, presumably at the thought of their failure to make their regular purchase from his father's store.

"No Joe – we can't stop today," Sylv chirruped.

"We have to get back to Dotty's – her dad's doing a firework display."

"Ah yes." Joe nodded with enthusiasm. "Mr Parsons came in to purchase his fireworks for the display at 12.15 today. Bought every firework in the shop."

The girls had rarely seen Joe this pleased. "Wow, your dad must have spent a fortune!" Sylv nudged Dotty.

Joe beamed. "Including our finest *Mega Rocket Mania'* Home Firework Selection," he gushed. "It seems he's really entered into the spirit of *Mr Fawkes'* special night this year. He's been putting the display together all afternoon. Yes, I believe it's going to be quite the spectacle."

"Mr Parsons also came in at 12.35 for a packet of Starburst," Joe continued. "Then at 1.15 for a newspaper and a Kit Kat; then at 2.43 for a Curly Wurly, a packet of Monster Munch and a Mars Bar. Hungry work..." he mused. Dotty's dad was not the slimmest of men and had a notoriously sweet tooth, often sneaking out to purchase illicit confectionery when Mrs Parsons was not paying attention. "He hasn't been in since so I'm guessing he's finished it now."

"Pity I have to work," Joe observed wistfully. "Still, I'll see it from the counter if I keep the door open." He eyed Dotty pointedly.

"You're very welcome to come, Joe, if you can get someone to cover the shop for you," said Dotty, taking the hint. Joe hadn't been invited but Dotty didn't mind. She was quite simply in too good a mood to begrudge an extra guest, and she liked Joe.

"I'll go ask Jazz," he said, and darted off.

Jazz was Joe's fourteen year old sister. She was permanently in a bad mood and far too busy filing her nails and sneaking out to visit the butcher's son, Gavin, to do anyone a favour, especially Joe, who she found a perpetual source of annoyance. It was much to the girls' surprise, then, that Joe returned a moment later with a jar of Black Jacks and a grin.

"She says she'll do it!" Catching their expression Joe winked and tapped the side of his nose theatrically, the grin breaking into a chuckle.

"Jazz'll have been sneaking out again then!" Sylv sniggered, elbowing Dotty as she did so. The pair giggled. Together the three blazed out of the shop, running the final fifty yards to Dotty's.

It was a small party that huddled in the by now rather wet back garden of Dotty's house: just Dotty and her dad, Sylv and Sylv's dad, little Joe Raman and Dotty's next door neighbours, Rita and Reggie Davis. The Davises had been invited by default on account of the fact that they were the Parsons' only other immediate neighbours and that their gardens were therefore adjoining. In truth, no-one really liked the Davises very much though.

Joe's musings had been right: Dotty's dad had spent much of the afternoon building a bold display out of the fireworks bought from Eddie's, the *Mega Rocket Mania 'King Mega Rocket'* taking pride of place in the centre of the display.

"Congratulations, Mr Parsons, Sir," said Joe formally. "A display to be proud of. Do you mind if I take a closer look at your fabulous efforts, Sir?"

"Sure, Joe, if you like," said Dotty's dad. "Just don't touch anything," he cautioned. "Took me ages, you know."

Joe didn't answer. He was already busy reading the instructions on the back of the now empty *'King Mega Rocket'* display box.

Sylv's dad was showing the girls how to write their names in the air with sparklers, Mrs Davis all the time tutting: "Careful now, girls. Fireworks are deadly things, mind," and giving Sylv's dad dark looks when she thought the girls weren't watching (They had never got on ever since Sylv's mum had left, though Dotty didn't know why).

"Let them have their fun, Rita, they're fine," counselled Mr Davis.

Mrs Davis shot Mr Davis a dark look too, and pursed her lips. "I'll go and help Gwennie," she snapped, referring to Dotty's mum, and stalked off into the kitchen, shooting Sylv's dad one final extra-dark look as she went.

Dotty's mum was inside pretending to check on the jacket potatoes, although everyone knew she was really fussing over her dogs, a couple of elderly and ill-tempered pugs named Chip and Pin, on account that they were afraid of fireworks. She caught Dotty's eye and waved through the kitchen window, mouthing "Hiya, Dot!" from behind the glass.

"Hiya, Mam!" Dotty waved and beamed excitedly.

Dotty's dad made some final adjustments to the display, huffing and puffing and fretting and muttering about inclement weather as he did so. "Hope they light, could be a damp squib, like."

Then came the announcement: "Okay, folks, I think we're ready to go," he wheezed.

There was a ripple of excitement in the modest yard. Dotty squeezed Sylv's hand tightly.

They waited. Nothing happened. Dotty's dad seemed to be having difficulty getting the first firework to light. He fumbled with an increasingly damp box of matches, muttering something about the fuse being wet. The drizzle turned slowly into rain. An eternity passed.

"Sorry, folks, I'm going to have to go inside and find a lighter," he said, and lumbered toward the kitchen door.

"Can't we do something?" Dotty asked Sylv, exasperated. "If the fireworks don't light soon, we're going to be rained off."

"My mam said never to play with fireworks," cautioned Sylv. "You don't know what might happen."

At that moment Mr Davis sprang into action. "Now don't you worry yourselves, girls, let's see if we can work some Davis magic while Dotty's dad looks for a lighter." The girls eyed each other, and then Mr Davis, incredulously.

"I have a bad feeling about this, Dotty," whispered Sylv nervously.

And then it happened. It was all over in a flash (and a bang), although everything seemed to be in slow motion. Mr Davis knelt down to light one of the rockets. Dotty's dad must have seen him out of the kitchen window and ran to the glass, shouting and waving his arms.

"Reggie! Joe's in the way… Joe, watch out! Reggie, NOoooooo!!!!"

The rocket spluttered and faltered, and then there was a spark. Little Joe Raman was thrown backwards, his foot knocking the rocket stand as he fell, leaving the *King Mega Rocket* precariously angled towards the house. With a whizz and a cackle, the rocket set off. But instead of flying high into the air as it should have done, with a loud crack the huge firework made a bee line straight for the open kitchen door. There was the loudest clap of thunder Dotty had ever heard and a lot of smoke. Then the fire started. After that all Dotty could remember was the wail of fire engines and a lot of confusion.

There was nothing anyone in the garden (Dotty included) could have done to prevent the blaze. "Thank heavens there weren't more casualties," they said; though Dotty felt three adults and two dogs were quite enough, under the circumstances. And so it was that for the first time in her life Dotty was completely alone: without her mum or dad and without Chip and Pin. Dotty was scared and lonely. But the very worst thing was not the loneliness at all: it was that everyone insisted on calling her Dorothea. At home Dotty had only ever been called by her full name when she was in big trouble; now she felt like she was alone, and in big trouble, all of the time.

Never Play with Fireworks

Chapter 1

New Beginnings

In which Dotty travels to Yorkshire and meets a mad lady at the station

"I can't believe they've done this to me!" wailed Dotty, pulling an oversized handkerchief from her jean pocket and blowing hard.

"Mind my ears, Dotty; you sound like a herd of elephants trumpeting away. And where did you get that filthy rag from?" Sylv grimaced.

"It was Dad's." More tears. Dotty had bought the monogrammed handkerchief for her dad as a birthday present a few years ago. She was just learning her letters and had insisted on buying the one with a letter 'D' on it (for 'Dad') even though her father's name was Brian. Her father had carried it everywhere he went. The handkerchief reminded Dotty of her dad. Everything reminded Dotty of her dad; and of her mum too, for that matter.

Dotty and Sylv were Skyping– it was the first time they had spoken since Dotty's move 'Up North', although that wasn't surprising as Dotty had only arrived at her new home ten minutes before. Both girls were sitting on their beds: Sylv at her mum's and Dotty in her grand and vacuous bedroom in the strange new house in which she had come to live.

"Come on now, Dotty, this is unlike you. Dry your eyes. I'm going to be bored stupid all holidays and I'm relying on you to tell me something interesting. So tell me all about this mansion you're living in. And tell me all about your Great Uncle Winchester. Have you met him yet?"

It hadn't been easy for Dotty since the fire. Concerned smiles seemed to fly at her from all angles, making her want to run and hide. The grown-ups all kept sighing and tutting, and saying "nine is too young to lose your parents." Dotty could not think of any age when losing one's parents was appropriate but, nevertheless, she definitely agreed that nine and a half was not it. And as if this tragic loss wasn't enough, it seemed the grown-ups were intent on making Dotty's life more miserable still by moving her away from her home in Cardiff to go and live with her mother's uncle in deepest, darkest Yorkshire: an area of the country she had no knowledge of, nor ever wished to discover.

Dotty had been given a brief reprieve from her Yorkshire sentence. As the winter term had not yet ended, the grown-ups thought it would be less disruptive if Dotty continued at school until then. So it had been agreed with Sylv's Dad that she would stay with them until the start of the Christmas holidays. Dotty found it difficult coming home from school every day to see the burnt-out shell that had been her family home since she was born. The scene of the fire served as a stark reminder of the accident that had so cruelly taken her parents from her, but Dotty told herself that at least she was in a familiar place with her best friend, and she found some strange sort of comfort in being close to home.

But now the holidays were about to start and there was no further room for delay. Sylv had to go and stay with her mum in Bristol, leaving Dotty with no choice but to make the move up to Yorkshire to start her new life there. Sylv had promised to write. "We can Skype all the time," she said. "And 'phone. And email. And my dad says you can visit any time." But it wouldn't be the same. Dotty was devastated. The adults insisted it was a good thing, that it would give her time to settle in over Christmas before she started a new school in January. Dotty did not agree. As far as she was concerned she was being moved to what might as well be the other side of the world forever and no amount of good timing could fix that.

As for Great Uncle Winchester, she had never met him before. In fact, prior to the accident, she wasn't even aware her mum *had* an Uncle Winchester.

"Oh, Sylv, it's awful: just awful." Dotty took a big gulp of air between sobs, distraught.

"It's big, and it's creepy, and it's dark and it's cold and…well, it's in *Yorkshire!*" More sobs.

"Yeah but it's a mansion, Dot. That has to be just a little bit cool, right?"

"It's not *our* mansion though is it, Sylv?"

Back in Cardiff, the girls liked to pretend that the two halves of the modest building that formed Sylv and Dotty's parents' semi's was their very own 'mansion house', as they called it – with Dotty living in the 'West Wing' and Sylv in the 'East'. The two houses were a mirror image of each other inside, which meant that Dotty and Sylv's bedrooms were next to each other, with only a paper thin wall between them. The girls took great delight in talking to each other every night through the bedroom wall, using a glass. Skype was better, of course, because she could actually see Sylv, but secretly Dotty somehow preferred communicating through the glass. "The old fashioned ways are best," as her mum had used to say. Dotty looked down and fiddled with a corner of her handkerchief, trying not to cry.

"Oh, Sylv, I just know I'm going to hate it here."

Sylv put on her stern face. "Right, now that's enough, Dotty Parsons. You've gotta be more positive. You've got a whole new world to explore up there and it'll be ages till I get up to visit you, so I need you to tell me all about it."

"Well you know I'd only just arrived, Sylv, when you Skyped me," Dotty countered defensively. "I haven't seen anything, 'cept my bedroom really."

It was true. Sylv had made a solemn oath to Dotty to stay in touch on Skype and sure enough as promised the icon on Dotty's iPad had started flashing almost as soon as she had got into the house.

"Well you can start with that, then, can't you?" Sylv insisted. "Is that a four poster bed you're sitting on? It looks amazing! I bet the whole place is absolutely lush."

Dotty pulled a tortured face and rolled her eyes. "Okay, you win. I'll tell you what I know."

*

If Dotty was already less than enthusiastic at the prospect of moving to Yorkshire, the journey up there had done little to change her mind. It was a damp, dreary December day. Not raining, but cold and dark; the sort of day that makes you want to stay under the bed covers and eat buttered crumpets.

New Beginnings

The journey Up North was to be by train, Great Uncle Winchester being unavailable to drive down to Wales to fetch Dotty because of some pressing business he had to attend to at home. Instead, Dotty's great uncle was to meet her off the train at Leeds. Sylv's dad had driven Dotty to the train station, together with her luggage, which didn't consist of a great deal because of the fire.

She had a small rucksack containing her few new clothes, her iPad (a present from Great Uncle Winchester so that the girls could keep in touch) and her treasured roller blades. Even they had only happened to survive the fire because Dotty's mum insisted they were kept in the front porch: the one part of the house that had avoided the worst of the blaze, thank goodness.

The four-hour journey dragged. The weather worsened. Dotty tried to read a book but she couldn't concentrate. She had no idea where Yorkshire was. Her old schoolteacher, Miss Tribble, had helped her look it up on a map, although all Dotty could sensibly discern from this was that it seemed a very long way away from Cardiff.

Dotty's mind kept veering off to thoughts of this strange place: Yorkshire, the house and Great Uncle Winchester. Her heart raced. What would it be like? What would *he* be like? What would school be like? She hoped they had a netball team. Dotty drifted off into an uneasy but much needed sleep at round about the time the train was passing through Nottingham, and there her worried daydreams turned into a turbulent sea of changing predictions about her future.

She awoke at Leeds with a gentle squeeze on the shoulder from a friendly train guard: a lady with thick blond hair cut just short of her shoulders, and a kind smile.

"You're in Leeds now, love. Time to get off the train."

Dotty glanced out of the train window, her eyes quickly scanning the platform for anyone who might be Great Uncle Winchester. Instead, her gaze alighted upon a strange looking female figure on the concourse. Dotty blinked hard and then looked again. The woman, who was in the latter part of middle age, was making what could only be described as a complete spectacle of herself. She beamed from ear to ear like an over-excited schoolgirl and waved manically in Dotty's direction. Dotty eyed her suspiciously. The woman was short in stature – no more than five feet tall – and matronly, with a mass of wiry curls that tumbled out at all angles from her white cloth mop-cap: the type you see maids wearing in the mid-afternoon Victorian melodramas Dotty's mum had liked to watch on TV. The woman's face was round (as was the rest of her) and rather red around the nose and cheeks – too many hours standing over a steaming stock pot, Dotty reckoned, for this person was clearly a cook.

It was not just the cap that gave Dotty this impression. Over her plain brown dress the woman was wearing a large white cooking apron covered in flour (as was much of the rest of her), protruding from the front pocket of which was a rolling pin – also much floured. Dotty stared at the vision in flour again. Perhaps she was still dreaming. Clearly this person didn't belong in any sensible scene from modern life. The cook continued to wave.

Dotty had just concluded that she must be an over-zealous National Trust volunteer escaped from one of their annual Heritage Days, when she noticed something hanging around the woman's neck. It was a makeshift cardboard sign, with 'DOROTHEA PARSONS' scrawled on it in blue marker pen. *Well that blew the 'mad lady waiting for somebody else' theory out of the water then,* thought Dotty, miserably. Great Uncle Winchester must have sent her. Dotty stood up on the arm of the chair, blindly searching the luggage rack above her head for her rollerblades. "Here, let me help you with those," said the friendly guard. Dotty muttered her '*thank you*'s and stumbled off the train. She took one last look along the platform but by now everyone had alighted and the station was almost empty. The floury woman bounced towards her, arms outstretched.

"*Croeso i Yorkshire!*" the old Yorkshire woman welcomed Dotty in her very best schoolgirl Welsh. "Oh, my dear, how pleased we are to have you at the Calendar House," she said, enveloping Dotty in a floury hug. "My name is Mrs Gobbins."

Dotty had to admit that, if nothing else, Mrs Gobbins smelled good. Her whole being seemed to emanate the aroma of freshly baked currant buns. Contrary to her somewhat disconcerting 'straight out of a storybook' appearance, her fragrance was admittedly rather pleasing, and Dotty might even have gone so far as to say it was comforting, was it not for the woman's constant chattering.

"Oh my poor lamb, listen to me babbling on," she continued. "What a long journey you must have had. Let's get you home." At that Mrs Gobbins turned on her heel and headed off at a surprisingly agile pace towards the station exit.

Dotty hurried along behind her new acquaintance, struggling to keep up. Her rollerblades, the laces of which she had tied together and put around her neck for ease of carrying, kept clashing together and strangling her. Dotty had put her iPad safely in her rucksack but this made it a little too heavy and the straps kept slipping off her shoulders. She tripped and struggled forwards, trying not to lose the speedy cook. Mrs Gobbins seemed not to notice. After a further small internal panic: *'oh please let her be driving us home in a car, not on a horse and cart, or a motorbike and side car, or anything else in the least embarrassing,'* Dotty caught up to the woman just as she alighted next to the strangest looking car Dotty had ever seen.

The car was a Citroen; Dotty knew that because her dad had always driven Citroens and she recognised the two arrow-like flashes on the bonnet of the car. Other than that, the vehicle was pretty much unrecognisable alongside any of its modern counterparts. The quaint old Citroen 2CV Dolly (*well at least it's a car,* Dotty reasoned), was red and white, with a red and white stripy cloth roof that looked like it had been borrowed from a deck chair. It had big bug-eyed headlights and curvy fenders and looked altogether friendly, not unlike Mrs Gobbins herself, had she been sporting a red and white striped dress.

"Quickly now, child," Mrs Gobbins busied herself adjusting the driver's seat. "Hop in. We have a way to go before we get there, and I have a pot on the boil."

Dotty did as she was told. She strapped herself in to the red upholstered armchair-like passenger seat and they set off. The car creaked and swayed like a ship in the wind. Everything rattled.

"Now, dear, we must be formally introduced. As I told you on the platform I am Mrs Gobbins, but what should I call you? My name plate here," she rapped her cardboard chest-plate with her knuckles, swerving to narrowly miss a pedestrian as she did so "says your name is Dorothea but, no offence to your blessed mother, God rest her soul, and I'm sure you'll grow into it in time…" (Dotty wondered if Mrs Gobbins was going to take a breath soon), "but that seems like an awfully big name for a little scrap like you. Would you mind if I called you Dotty?"

And all of a sudden Dotty decided that Mrs Gobbins was really rather nice.

"Mrs Gobbins, what is the Calendar House?" Dotty ventured, "And where is Great Uncle Winchester?"

"The Calendar House?" Mrs Gobbins exclaimed. "My goodness don't you know? Did your mother never mention it? Why it's the great Winchester family home! Owned by generations of Winchesters. It was the childhood home of your mother and now it'll be your home too." Mrs Gobbins smiled generously at Dotty.

On the hour-long journey from the train station, above the shaking and rattling of the precarious Citroen Dolly, Mrs Gobbins told Dotty all about her mother's family. They were reputed to have made their fortune in the coal mining industry; although what Great Uncle Winchester did Dotty was not exactly sure. Mrs Gobbins said he worked in the family business, so Dotty assumed he must have something to do with coal.

Dotty was so busy listening to all Mrs Gobbins had to say that she hadn't been paying attention to the journey at all. But now, suddenly, she was aware of being on gravel. They had turned into the driveway of the house. It had become quite dark but nevertheless Dotty could make out the outline of a mansion house, tall and grand, sprawling out in every direction from large, solid double front doors. The doorway was lit by a singularly large carriage lamp that swayed uneasily above it, creaking and groaning under its own great weight in the wind. It was imposing, to say the least.

"Here we are, Dotty," chirped Mrs Gobbins. "Out you hop."

*

"The house is really interesting, Sylv," continued Dotty in her description of her newly discovered family home. "Gobby says," (the girls had already given the cook a nickname, on account of her name so aptly matching her innate ability to talk ninety-to-the-dozen) "it has three hundred and sixty-five rooms, fifty-two chimneys, four wings. So it has a North and a South wing, Sylv, as well as an East and a West." Sylv looked suitably impressed. "And it has seven staircases too. So it's just like a real calendar. I'm going to try and visit all the rooms before I start school in the New Year."

"Wow, Dotty, that's awesome," said Sylv. "Although, hang on a minute: that means you'll

Chapter 1

have to visit at least twenty rooms per day, by my reckoning. You'll never do it!"

Sylv had always been better at maths than Dotty. "Well I've got nothing better to do, have I?" she pouted. "And it beats listening to Gobby *gobbing* all day long."

"Don't put her down, Dotty, that woman's a real catch. I bet you anything she makes you cakes and biscuits and all sorts. I have to say I'm quite jealous." Sylv's dad was no natural cook and the best her mum ever came up with was about-to-go-out-of-date Mr Kipling whenever they appeared in the bargain bin at the local supermarket. A vet by trade, when Sylv stayed with her mum in Bristol, her mum was usually too busy rescuing some distressed animal or other to notice she even had a daughter, let alone bake her a cake.

Dotty pulled a sour face, impatient with her friend's preoccupation with her stomach. "Well?" she snapped. "Do you want to hear about the house or not?"

"Yes, yes, Dotty, go on." Sylv folded her hands in her lap, waiting patiently.

"To be honest, Sylv, I don't have a whole lot more to tell you right now, except that my bedroom's massive, as you can see, and I've got a four poster bed."

"Just like a princess out of a fairy story," Sylv teased.

Dotty stuck out her tongue. "Anyway, I've gotta go. Gobby told me to wash up: supper in five minutes." A bell rang in the distance. "That'll be her now."

"Hang on, Dot, before you go, you haven't told me about your Great Uncle Winchester."

Dotty shrugged. "He wasn't here when I arrived. Gobby says I'm going to meet him tomorrow morning at eleven."

Chapter 2

Waiting for Winchester

In which Dotty explores her new home and meets a monster

Dotty had a surprisingly good night's sleep, considering it was her first night in her new home. Gobby had treated Dotty to an early supper in the kitchen: creamy scrambled eggs with chunky bread soldiers as thick as they were wide, topped with lashings of fresh butter. And so it was that with a full stomach and already sleepy eyes Dotty was marched off up the back stairs to the nursery bathroom (so entitled by Gobby).

There, despite Dotty's ample protestations, the cook proceeded to run her a hot bath in an impossibly huge old fashioned bath tub that filled the centre of the room. After some initial choking and spluttering of the pipes, the boat of a bath filled surprisingly quickly and before very long it was overflowing with the sweetest smelling bubbles: scents of tangerines and jasmine filling the room. It was difficult to resist.

After a "long hot soak in the tub," (as Dotty's mum would have said), Dotty donned a pair of thick flannelette pyjamas, laid out for her by Gobby, and at last was able to crawl under the covers of the four poster bed that dominated the bedroom.

"I've put your clothes away in the dresser by the fireplace, Dotty," said Gobby, "and there's a glass of hot milk by the bed. I've sweetened it with a little honey." She smiled knowingly. "It'll help you sleep. Now, would you like your curtains closing?"

Dotty looked, puzzled, at the heavy drapes that covered the window. "But, Mrs Gobbins, they're already closed."

"No dear, I meant your bed curtains," she said, pulling out some heavily patterned brocade from the side of the bed frame. "They stop the draft from getting under the covers. You need them in a big old house like this."

Dotty was past arguing and Gobby's reasoning sounded logical so she did not protest. As Gobby pulled the curtains around the four poster, Dotty felt the dark and the warmth enveloping her. She put down the milk glass that she had previously clasped in her hand and tucked her chin well under the covers. Without further ado the cook bade her goodnight.

"Sleep tight, Dotty, my dear." Gobby gave Dotty a light peck on the forehead and almost melted out of the room on those surprisingly speedy and agile feet.

As she drifted off to sleep, Dotty gazed at the pattern on the thick brocade in the dim remaining light. Her first thought was that the curtains were floral in pattern, but now she fancied there were tiny figures playing on them. What were they now? They appeared to be… could they be… chimney sweeps?

Dotty woke early, eager to explore the house. She pulled on a pair of jeans and a thick grey woollen jumper with a big pocket in the front and toyed with the idea of donning her roller blades. This was a large house, after all, and it would add speed to her explorations. But thinking better of it for her first expedition she pulled on a pair of slipper socks instead.

Much of what Dotty was wearing was not hers: or, rather, Dotty thought it must be hers but she had not brought it with her. The dresser was jam-packed full of clothing just the right size for a nine and a half year old girl. She assumed Gobby must have bought it for her, knowing that much of her own clothing had been lost to the fire. The cook was a thoughtful old bird, if a bit quirky, Dotty thought.

Waiting for Winchester

It was 7.15 a.m. Dotty pulled open the heavy bedroom drapes and looked out into the eerie morning light. For a brief moment she watched the first mist rising from the moor in the distance. Then tripping down the back steps and in to the kitchen, she found Gobby already busying herself, merrily humming some unrecognisable tune.

Dotty's eyes came at once to rest on a rather precarious but wonderfully scented pile of freshly baked Welsh cakes, still steaming on the hot plate. Grabbing a couple, Dotty pocketed one and shoved the other unceremoniously into her mouth, whilst simultaneously making a quick dash towards the kitchen door. There was a lot to do before eleven o'clock and her first meeting with Great Uncle Winchester.

"My! Aren't you in a hurry this morning," remarked Gobby, cheerily. "I hope you like the Welsh cakes." She eyed the crummy evidence peeking out of Dotty's jumper pocket. "I made them especially. I thought they might remind you of home. I expect your mother cooked them all the time, did she?" The old cook smiled benignly.

Dotty didn't like to say they almost never ate Welsh cakes in her household; and those that they did eat certainly weren't home made by her mum. They were more likely to be bought from the local Tesco's or from Eddie's on the corner. But Dotty appreciated the sentiment anyway.

"Now then, Dotty, what are you going to do today?" Gobby continued, not waiting for an answer to the Welsh cake question.

"I'm going to take a look around the house, if that's okay, Mrs Gobbins," said Dotty.

"Yes of course, poppet, you take your time and explore. There's plenty to see, but mind you don't get lost," the cook added. "And don't get too close to the fireplaces." She frowned and wagged a finger for emphasis.

Dotty smiled. Gobby's warning about the danger of open fires was kindly and sweet and reminded her of one of her mother's little quirks. Just like Gobby, Dotty's mum had always got a bit jumpy when she ventured too near to an open fireplace, even when there was no fire lit. As for getting lost, whilst Dotty could easily imagine losing her way in a house as large as this one, she had a good sense of direction and, quite frankly the idea simply added to the excitement of her exploring it. She trotted off merrily to do just that.

According to Gobby, Great Uncle Winchester did not have any children of his own. For that matter, he did not have a wife, nor any other family except for Dotty. The result was that the house was very empty, with few comings and goings as far as Dotty could tell, and she was left to roam the house undisturbed. On the ground floor (for that was where Dotty had started her exploration) the doors were closed but so far unlocked, opening onto a series of large formal rooms, vast and high ceilinged, with pictures of nameless ladies and gentlemen from a forgotten era adorning the walls (Were they ancestors of hers, she wondered?). Most of the rooms were obviously unused, as the furniture was covered in dust sheets. Dotty tried to form a mental picture of the layout of the house as she visited each room, but all too soon she had lost track.

Darting turned to trudging as Dotty traipsed up and down the house's endless corridors. There was a great old library, big enough that it could fit the whole of Dotty's house in Cardiff within its walls, she imagined, and filled with dusty old tomes - but not a Jacqueline Wilson in sight. There was a room full of plates that Dotty rather liked, their colourful and intricate designs covering the walls from floor to ceiling, although she couldn't really see the purpose of such a room. And there was a pretty drawing room with wallpaper alive with exotic birds and doors leading through a glass house and out onto the formal garden. *Mental note to explore the garden later*, Dotty thought.

The architectural niceties of the house were of little interest to a girl of Dotty's age. The only thing she really noticed about the rooms was the vast fireplaces that dominated them. You could easily step into them and Dotty imagined that, if you did, a girl her size could be easily sucked up and away to goodness knows where if they weren't careful. Perhaps that was what her mum and Gobby were afraid of, Dotty smiled in spite of herself.

The designs on the fireplaces were incredibly intricate, depicting scenes and stories in their marble surrounds so detailed that they seemed almost to have a life of their own. As the light and shadow danced upon them Dotty even fancied that the figures were moving.

Dotty particularly liked the fireplace in the 'Bird Room' as she called it, and she lingered there for a moment to take a better look at it. The fire surround depicted a boy and girl standing facing one another to the right and left of the fire, bending forwards, their heads almost touching in the middle as if they were about to embrace.

Suddenly unable to resist the urge, Dotty stepped off the hearth from where she had been standing to examine the fire, and in one small stride walked straight into the open fireplace. Standing perfectly still Dotty looked up into the darkness. She couldn't see the sky through the top of the chimney. In fact all she could see was an ever-extending blackness above her. She wondered where it went.

Leaving the Bird Room Dotty continued in her search of the house. As she roamed the corridors she was surprised at how quickly she tired of the mysterious house and all its secrets, although she did make a mental note that it would be a great place to play hide and seek, should she ever have a friend to visit.

And then it struck her. This was the reason she felt so very sad, the thing that was at the heart of the problem with her morning's exploring: she was alone. Even the greatest of adventures meant nothing when you had no-one to share it with. Now feeling suddenly despondent, Dotty slowly made her way back through the house, enthusiasm for her great new adventure fading rapidly with every step.

But then, as Dotty trudged wearily back towards the kitchen, she noticed a door that she hadn't previously seen. It was because when she was walking the length of the corridor in the opposite direction, this door would have been on the left of the corridor, whereas the other doors were all on the right. This seemed odd. Surely it meant that the room would be on the inside of the house, rather than facing out onto the garden like the others?

Giving a little shrug as if to shake away the question Dotty tried the handle of the door. Like all the other doors she had so far come across, this one was unlocked. The door opened onto a room in darkness. Dotty remained unsure as to whether this was because the room had no window or simply whether the blind was still closed. Fumbling for a light switch, she strained her eyes and tried to focus. The room seemed to be a large untidy office of sorts, papers piled high on a sturdy oak desk. *Boring*, thought Dotty, and turned to leave the room without bothering to turn on the light.

But as she started to close the door her eye caught something moving in the corner in the dark. Struggling to see in the dim light her mind started to race. As quickly as her fear took hold the shadow took form. Dotty realized with little relief that the shadow was not the unearthly creature of her imagination but rather the form of a man, or something that resembled a man, albeit in a rather unearthly way. The man was tall and impossibly thin, with sharp weasel-like features, a pointed nose and protruding teeth barely covered by paper thin lips. His back was curved, bending forwards to make his reedy frame seem to form a perpetual human question mark.

The man-creature slunk out of the shadows, peering towards the girl from the darkness. His slim dark suit seemed only to emphasize his grotesque form.

"What are you doing in here?" the man demanded in a high-pitched whine of a voice that was almost as unnatural as his looks. "You are not allowed in here. Get out." His voice rose almost to a shriek in its displeasure. "I said get OUT!"

Dotty screamed and, turning on her heels, fled as quickly as her legs would take her, back towards the safety of Gobby and her kitchen.

Gobby was up to her eyes in flour again, now baking what looked like a flan of some sort.

"Oh, Mrs Gobbins, there's a monster in the house!" Dotty sobbed. "In a room. In a dark, dark room at the end of the corridor."

Gobby rubbed her hands on her apron, her face the picture of concern. "Calm yourself, child," she tutted soothingly. "Now what is all this about creatures in the dark?" Instinctually Gobby gathered Dotty to her breast and Dotty cuddled into her, breathing in her warm bread-bun smell. Dotty sobbed uncontrollably for a few minutes, the shock of her frightening experience giving vent to her deeper sadness. Then, taking a few deep breaths, she continued.

"Well, rather, it was a man. I mean, I think it was a man," Dotty stuttered. "He was in a big dark room, like an office. He shouted at me." Dotty hid her face in her hands, wracked with sobs.

Suddenly Gobby became very serious. She moved back a pace to look at Dotty, searching her eyes for the truth of the matter. "Now, Dotty, what did this man look like?"

As Dotty described the strange man, Gobby's face eased. "I see. Well, Dotty, your monster is none other than your Great Uncle Winchester's private secretary. His name is Mr. Strake."

Gobby smiled, dropping her shoulders with the relief of the discovery. "Don't you trouble yourself with him, poppet. Mr Strake is nothing to be afraid of although I'll grant you he does look a little odd." She busied herself wiping tears from Dotty's tear-stained face. "Now, let's stop that crying and give me a nice big *cwtch*. We'll have no tears in my kitchen." This was the second time Gobby had spoken to Dotty in Welsh since her arrival in Yorkshire and the old cook's use of the colloquial Welsh term for 'cuddle' seemed strange coming from her mouth. It was comforting, nevertheless, and Dotty relaxed; her breathing became less rapid and her sobs more shallow.

After a little time had passed, Gobby ventured a new question of Dotty. "So, apart from Great Uncle Winchester's study, where else have you been so far this morning? Have you visited the upstairs of the house yet?"

"I've been downstairs, just downstairs." Dotty looked questioningly at Gobby, her curiosity piqued. She had imagined the upstairs to be the least interesting part of the house, thinking it would just be full of musty old bedrooms, but Gobby obviously knew differently.

"Well, perhaps you've had enough exploring for one day, but I do think there's something up there that you might like to see. I wonder if you might like to take a look at your mother's playroom."

Dotty's face lit up. "Really? Mam's old playroom? It's still here? In the house?"

But before Dotty could ask any more questions and before Gobby could have answered, the kitchen clock bonged noisily, making the cook jump to her feet in exclamation.

"Oh my goodness is that really the time? Come on Dotty, you have to get going. You are going to be late to meet your great uncle."

It seemed that Mam's Playroom would just have to wait until later.

Chapter 3

Great Uncle Winchester

In which Dotty finally meets her great uncle and is promised a new friend

"Get going?" Dotty was perplexed. "But get going where, Mrs Gobbins? Where on earth *is* Great Uncle Winchester?"

"Why of course your great uncle will be in his study, Dotty." Gobby started to usher Dotty towards the open kitchen door. "Now run along, you're late already."

"But I don't know where the study is!" Dotty whined.

"Of course you do!" Gobby looked at Dotty in surprise. "You've been there once already this

27

morning. Your Great Uncle Winchester's study is where you met Mr. Strake."

Dotty went pale. "Strake!" she stuttered, "*That's* where he was? Won't he still be there?" Dotty knotted her hands, now a little less keen to see her great uncle.

"Oh pish-posh, Dotty," the ample cook scolded. "I told you, there's nothing fearsome about that man. He can't do anything to hurt you."

"But I think he might want to," Dotty mumbled, shuffling from foot to foot and hanging her head.

Gobby began herding Dotty up the vast expanse of corridor. "Now don't you fret, dear. I'll tell you what: I'll walk you there myself." And without further ado Gobby set off down the hallway, leaving a floury trail behind her as evidence of her recent flan-making, and walking at such a pace that Dotty practically had to run the length of the corridor to keep up.

To Dotty's great relief, when they reached Great Uncle Winchester's study her fears were proved unfounded. Strake was nowhere to be seen and neither was the gloomy half-light from whence he had appeared. In fact, the room was almost unrecognisable from when Dotty had seen it barely an hour previously. The heavy door was flung open wide in welcome and light flooded in from the tall window that stood behind the desk. There was a muslin blind across the window frame obscuring the view beyond, but this did not prevent the sunshine from pouring through it onto the vast array of books that lay upon the table. The books did not just cover the desk: Dotty now saw that they also lay in piles and piles over almost every inch of floor space and each and every other flat surface in the room.

Dotty stared in wonder at the haphazard scene. Piles of papers balanced from floor to ceiling at every imaginable angle. Mesmerised for a moment, she pondered how these dog-eared tomes managed to remain upright, if not balanced by some exterior force. There was no sign of Great Uncle Winchester though.

For the second time that morning Dotty turned to leave the office. But as she did so she noticed a faint humming that appeared to be coming from the far right hand corner of the room. Gripped by fear that it might be Strake, Dotty whirled around looking for Gobby, but the cook had disappeared, determined to return to the kitchen and her baking as quickly as she had left it. The humming grew louder. "Hmm, hmm, hum, hum, hummMMM."

As bravely as she dared, Dotty turned to face the room once more. "Hello?" she ventured in a small voice. "Great Uncle Winchester?"

The humming stopped. All of a sudden, out from behind a particularly precarious stack of books (in a far less sinister and alarming fashion than Strake had done) popped Great Uncle Winchester.

"Dorothea, my dear girl!" he boomed. "Finally we meet." He bounded across the room and in three great strides he had reached her, hands outstretched in greeting. Several of the book piles wobbled as he did so. Dotty resisted the urge to duck. As he came towards her, the light framed the old man's white hair like a halo around his head. "So pleased: so pleased, dear girl." Great Uncle Winchester grabbed Dotty's hand in both of his, shaking it enthusiastically as he talked. "Well my goodness, aren't you just a picture? It's so good to meet you at last."

Serious for a moment, Great Uncle Winchester stopped shaking and held Dotty's captured hand. "My darling girl, I was so sorry to hear about your mother," he squeezed her hand gently, "and your father, of course."

A moment of silence. "But now you must tell me all about yourself. We have a lot of catching up to do." Great Uncle Winchester was all smiles again and it was hard for Dotty not to follow his lead, such was the aura of happiness that exuded from him at all angles, a little like his piles of books.

Winchester was a robust man with rosy cheeks and a kind smile and, as it turned out, a seemingly never ending source of mint humbugs in his pocket that he did not mind sharing. His wild white hair and cherubic features Dotty would have thought gave him an air of St Nicholas were it not for the absence of a beard, although his huge bushy white sideburns almost singularly made up for the lack of hair on his chin.

Dotty surveyed her great uncle closely. She could at once see the family resemblance: he had her mother's smile and at that moment the quizzical expression she often wore. Dotty liked him immediately. He was the sort of person it was difficult not to like.

Great Uncle Winchester's clothes were as exuberant as his personality. Dotty saw that he was wearing mustard coloured knickerbockers, a woollen waistcoat and a green tweed jacket. She wondered if he was about to play golf.

"Aha, I see you are admiring my golfing attire, Dorothea," grinned her great uncle. "Do you have an interest in the sport my dear? It's not just for boys, you know: it's just as much a girls' game as it is for us chaps." He swung an imaginary golf club through the air by way of illustration.

Dotty stared at him, bemused. It wasn't that she had thought golf to be a sport reserved exclusively for boys; it was that she thought it was a game reserved exclusively for old people.

Great Uncle Winchester waved the golfing image away. "Anyway, I digress. Now come and sit with me by the fire and tell me all there is to know about Dorothea Parsons. I say, would you care for a humbug?"

Dotty and Great Uncle Winchester slipped into easy conversation. Her great uncle was everything Dotty didn't expect him to be. She had imagined a shy, retiring, quiet man who locked himself away in his study and preferred not to be around children. She couldn't have been more wrong. Great Uncle Winchester was fun. Great Uncle Winchester loved children. In spirit, at least, Great Uncle Winchester was no more than a child himself.

As they sat by the fire, Dotty found herself telling her newly found confidant all about home, and her parents, and Sylv and Chip and Pin the dogs, and she talked about how lonely she had been since the fire, all the while her uncle tutting and nodding and feeding her humbugs. Dotty told him just how lost she felt without them all, although as they talked she had to admit, to herself at least, that for the first time since it had happened she actually didn't feel too bad.

Their conversation was interrupted by a curt knock at the door. Feeling herself in shadow, Dotty turned around to find Strake looming in the doorway, a heavily laden tea tray in hand.

"Your lunch, Sir," Strake simpered making a grimace that Dotty surmised was supposed to approximate a smile. She felt a small involuntary shudder. Strake gave her the creeps.

Chapter 3

Great Uncle Winchester was unperturbed. "Ah excellent, Strake. Do put it down on the desk for me." Strake shuffled into the room and Dotty watched him as he struggled to find a space upon which to place the tray.

"Mr. Winchester, Sir. Begging your pardon but there is the small matter of some papers to attend to. Quite urgent, Sir, and needing your immediate attention, if you don't mind." Having relieved himself of the tea tray, Strake tapped his wrist watch as he spoke.

"Yes, yes, Strake. There's no need to remind me. Don't you think a man can remember his own business?" Great Uncle Winchester growled, waving Strake away as if shooing away a fly. As he did so, Dotty noticed her great uncle was wearing a large ring on his little finger: gold and black, with a strange symbol on it. Could it be a broom?

Strake slunk out of the room without another word looking suitably wounded, closing the door behind him by way of a full stop. The uncomfortable atmosphere left the room with him.

Great Uncle Winchester turned to Dotty. "I'm afraid Strake is right, though. It is time for me to take my leave of you for today." Dotty's face fell. "In any event, I expect Mrs Gobbins will be calling you for your lunch any moment soon and I have to eat mine too. You can't do business on an empty stomach, you know."

Dotty eyed the tea tray, suppressing a giggle. It was an impressive spread, even by Gobby's standards. Apart from the large pot of steaming tea, cup and saucer, milk, and a generous bowl of sugar lumps, the tray contained a plate of biscuits (jammy dodgers: Dotty's favourite), a whole Battenberg cake, partially sliced, and what Dotty guessed were peanut butter sandwiches with the crusts cut off. Dotty hoped fervently that her own lunch resembled her great uncle's. Her stomach rumbled.

"There you are you see, Dorothea, you need your sustenance also." Her great uncle stood, prompting Dotty to do the same. "Now please don't fret, my darling girl. We will have plenty more time to chat, I swear. I have a little work I must finish off today but promise me you will come by my office tomorrow afternoon; there's someone really special who I'd like you to meet."

Dotty brightened. "Oh who, Great Uncle Winchester, who?" she asked excitedly.

"You'll see tomorrow, Dorothea. Someone who I think might be a friend to you. Now tell me you'll stop by my office at around two o'clock."

"Okay, Great Uncle Winchester, I will." And with that, a little saddened at their parting, but nevertheless intrigued, Dotty did as she was told and made for the kitchen.

Unfortunately lunch was not the sweet affair Dotty hoped it would be. She picked at her quiche salad with little enthusiasm. It wasn't that the flan was not nice; it was just that in a nine and a half year old's eyes it measured up poorly to her great uncle's lunch of biscuits and Battenberg. Dotty pushed a piece of cucumber around her plate miserably.

Gobby eyed Dotty with knowing suspicion. "I suppose your uncle's been feeding you humbugs," she harrumphed, less than pleased.

Dotty surveyed the cook's expression and thought better than to deny it. Instead, she decided to change the conversation to another less sensitive topic, by asking who Gobby thought it could be that Great Uncle Winchester planned to introduce her to the following day.

"How would I know?" Gobby was sadly unforthcoming, Dotty thought on account of her lack of enthusiasm for the cook's most recent food offering. "After all, I'm just the person who feeds you all around here." Gobby was clearly sulking and Dotty made a mental note to eat less humbugs at tomorrow's meeting with her great uncle. It seemed that she would just have to wait to find out who this mystery friend could be.

*

"Well your Great Uncle Winchester seems brilliant, but that Strake just sounds creepy to me." Sylv turned her nose up in disgust at the thought of him. "I'd stay well away from that one if I were you, Dotty."

Dotty and Sylv were Skyping again. Although it was only two in the afternoon, Dotty was tucked up comfortably within the folds of her four poster and its strangely patterned drapes: Dotty's self-appointed safe house and the best place to sit with your best friend and share secrets, she thought.

"I know, Sylv, but you should have seen Uncle Winchester wave him away, just like he was a servant or something, and he went. Just like that!"

"Good. Sounds like **wasn't all so bad** your uncle will keep him in check. Still, you be careful, Dot." Dotty nodded in agreement.

"So have you any idea who this person might be, the one your great uncle wants you to meet?" Sylv asked.

"Not a clue, Sylv. I'm pretty sure no one else lives here, and certainly nobody our age. Perhaps it's someone from the village." The small market town of Netherton lay two miles to the west of the Calendar House. Dotty hadn't been there yet but she knew that was where Gobby went to do the food shopping, and Dotty's school teacher, Miss Tribble, had shown it to her on the map when they talked about her, then imminent, move to Yorkshire.

"Well, promise me you'll give me a full report as soon as you are in the know. I don't want to miss out on any gossip." Sylv paused. "And promise me you won't let them take my place, Dotty. I miss you, you know." Suddenly Sylv looked a bit lost, frail almost. Dotty wished she could hug her.

"Nobody could ever take your place, Sylv," Dotty smiled at her best friend. "Pinky promise." She held her hand up to the screen of her iPad, little finger outstretched.

"Pinky promise, Dotty." Sylv did the same, eyes bright with tears.

"Anyway, I'm sure it will be someone super-boring," said Dotty reassuringly. "How are things at home, by the way?"

"Oh same as ever, Dot, you know how it is. Dad can't cope without me and is living on pre-packed sandwiches from Eddie's and Mum barely knows I'm here." Sylv rolled her eyes. "The flat is full of injured animals. There's a half-dead hamster in a cage in my room and Mum moved in a cat with an eating disorder yesterday. She says it has low self-esteem, whatever that means. The whole place stinks. I wish I could come and stay with you."

Poor Sylv. Since her parents had separated, Sylv had to spend all her holidays at her mum's flat in Bristol. The flat was conveniently placed above her mother's veterinary practice, but her work often over spilled into the flat itself, making for less than comfortable living. Dotty longed for a visit from her friend, but as Sylv was staying at her Mum's for the whole of the Christmas holidays it didn't look as if Dotty would be seeing her until Easter, which seemed an absolute lifetime away.

"I'm sure we can sort something out, Sylv. I'll talk to Great Uncle Winchester tomorrow. Perhaps you can come up at half term." Dotty stroked the screen, as if to reach out and touch her.

All at once there was a great calamity, yowls and squeaks emanating from the iPad. A skinny ginger cat streaked across the screen at speed. More squeaking followed.

"Sylv, what on earth is going on there?" Dotty was alarmed.

"Don't worry, Dot, it's just the cat escaping again and it's managed to get the hamster cage open." Sylv seemed relatively calm in the chaos. "Look, I'd better go. Big *cwtch*." Sylv signed off.

Dotty lay down on her bed, feeling suddenly tired from the morning's excitement, and from too many mint humbugs and a more than adequate lunch, which Gobby had salvaged at the last minute by producing a thick slice of Battenberg cake (but only once she had cleared her plate of quiche and salad).

She thought about her meeting with Great Uncle Winchester and imagined who it could be that she was supposed to be introduced to the following day. As she thought, it suddenly struck Dotty that for the whole of their conversation her great uncle had been calling her by her full name, Dorothea. And to her great surprise she realised that, for the first time in her life, she hadn't minded.

So it was that Dotty dozed and, for the first time since she had lost her parents, Dorothea Parsons could be found sleeping with the flicker of a smile on her face.

Great Uncle Winchester

Chapter 4

Jackdaws

In which Dotty discovers Mam's playroom and makes a lucky find

Perhaps it was because of her doze earlier that afternoon, but for one reason or another Dotty did not sleep well that night. In her broken sleep she kept on thinking she heard noises coming from her bedroom chimney.

At first she thought it was part of her imaginings as she drifted in and out of sleep. *Scritch scratch, scritch-scratch.* But somehow it seemed too persistent for that. *Scritch scratch, scritchety-scratch.* She wondered what it could be. A bird, perhaps? Or maybe mice? Dotty's sleep became more disturbed, waking and sleeping in equal measure, to the tune of the scritch-scratching of the chimney. It was annoying, if not enough to be alarming.

Dotty woke late. Too tired and befuddled to dress before breakfast, she trudged down the back stairs to the kitchen in a bit of a dream, hair askew, dressing gown more so. Breakfast was clearly over. The breakfast things had long since been cleared away, Dotty surmised, and Gobby was busy with the next round of baking for the day. It seemed that, despite the modest size of the household (although not of the house), the hard working cook was always kept busy preparing something. Whether it be bottled fruits or jams or a cake 'for the tin', there was always something going on.

Today, not altogether unusually, there was a thick dusting of flour over everything, including Gobby herself. The overwhelming scent of sweet spices filled the air. It smelled of Christmas, Dotty thought. Dotty had forgotten it was going to be Christmas soon. There were no decorations in the hallways of the big house nor was there a tree, swathed in twinkly lights to remind her of its coming. Dotty loved Christmas but her heart sank at the reminder: she couldn't imagine Christmas without her mum and dad, or Chip and Pin.

Gobby was mixing something in a huge earthenware bowl, puffing and blowing as she did so. Whatever she was making, it seemed to be very hard work. As Dotty stood at the doorway

Gobby stopped for a moment's rest, wiping a floury hand across her brow. The result was an equally floury face. Dotty giggled. "Ah, there you are," she said, not seeming to notice Dotty's dishevelled appearance. "You're just in time to make a wish."

"A wish?" asked Dotty.

"Yes, dear: in the pudding. I'm making the Christmas pudding for next year," replied Gobby a little impatiently, wiping a stray hair away from her cheek and adding yet more flour to her complexion.

"Next year's Christmas pudding?" Dotty was confused. "Don't you mean *this* year's Christmas pudding? And anyway, it's nearly a month until Christmas; isn't it too early to be making it yet?" she queried.

"It's only a fortnight 'til Christmas," retorted the cook. "And no, this is *next* year's pudding. I made this year's pudding last year. Did your mother not do this at home?"

This last comment was more of a statement than a question. "No," replied Dotty, deflated. Dotty's mum always bought her Christmas puddings from Tesco's, or Marks and Spencer's if they were 'feeling flush'. Dotty's dad didn't like Christmas pudding and her mum said there was no point making one just for the two of them. The truth was that Dotty's mum wasn't actually a very good cook and wasn't very organised either. The Old El Rango Mexican dinner kit range was a firm favourite in their household and as far as baking was concerned, making a Christmas pudding a year in advance would certainly have been outside the scope of her considerable skill set. There were always more important things to do in their household.

Realising her error, Gobby's face softened. "Well this will be an extra special treat then, won't it?" she said. "Come along and help me put the lucky sixpence in the cake." Gobby proffered a small silver coin.

Dotty hadn't seen a sixpence before and she eyed it with interest. "Why do you use a sixpence?" she asked.

"Oh tradition, dear, just tradition," Gobby answered gently. "Now then make a wish, Dotty, and throw it in the bowl."

Dotty clasped the sixpence, squeezing her eyes tight shut and wishing as hard as she could. She knew her wish could never come true, but Dotty wished it all the same. She threw the coin into the bowl of pudding batter, where it landed with a satisfying '*thwup*', then, capsizing, sank slowly into the thick brown goo of the mixture.

"Excellent, dear," commended Gobby with a satisfied nod. "Now, pass me that pudding basin and we'll get it cooking."

"Mrs Gobbins," asked Dotty as Gobby spooned the gloopy mixture into the pudding basin. "I kept hearing scratching in my room last night. It stopped me sleeping."

Gobby stopped her spooning and her eyes narrowed, just for a second. "I expect you were dreaming, Dotty. It is a big old house after all." The spooning continued.

"Yes I thought so too, at first, but now I'm sure it was real. It went on all night." The cook was concentrating very carefully on getting every last drop of batter out of the mixing bowl, scraping the bowl to within an inch of its life with her wooden spoon.

"I expect it was jackdaws, then." She eyed the empty bowl. *Scrape scrape*, went Gobby's spoon. *Scrapety-scrape*.

"Jackdaws?" Dotty asked.

"Yes, jackdaws." The mixing bowl was now scrupulously clean. "They nest on the chimney pots. Make a terrible mess. Filthy creatures."

Gobby pulled a face, picking up a circle of greaseproof paper and placing it over the top of the now full pudding basin. "Now, where did I put the string?"

Realising Gobby was not to be drawn on the subject, Dotty questioned her no further, but she found it hard to believe Gobby's account of the noise. After all, it was winter, and didn't birds make their nests in spring? Dotty was sure there must be another explanation for the scratching.

"Right then, that's ready for the pan." As if by magic, Gobby proudly produced a beautifully parcelled pudding, all tied up with string like a Christmas gift.

Dotty really wanted to sing a celebratory "Ta-dah!" but thought better of it. This was serious business to the cook.

Gobby lowered the pudding gingerly into a pot of boiling water that had been readying on the stove. "Three hours should do it." She nodded with satisfaction. "Oh, by the way, Dotty, your uncle left a letter for you." Gobby gestured to a slightly floury letter propped on one corner of the kitchen dresser against an oversized salt cellar.

"Thanks, Mrs Gobbins." Dotty snatched the letter, tearing it open as she did so. She wondered what her great uncle could want to tell her that couldn't wait until their meeting that afternoon.

Perhaps it would give her a clue as to the identity of Great Uncle Winchester's friend.

Eagerly, she opened the folded paper, keen to discover its contents. It read:

My Darling Girl,

So sorry but some urgent business has come up that I have to attend to in London. I am taking the early train this morning so I'm afraid I shall miss our meeting, but I do hope to be back in time to spend the Christmas celebrations with you.

With much love from your
Great Uncle Winchester

Chapter 4

p.s...

Dotty couldn't read any more: her eyes had filled with tears. She flung the letter down and ran blindly out of the kitchen. After everything she had been through to find such a welcome new confidant only to have him taken away so immediately, when she most needed a friend, seemed almost too much to bear.

Dotty didn't know where she was running, nor did she care much. She just needed to run. Dotty ran and ran and ran until there was nowhere left to run to, save for up a little flight of winding back stairs at the far end of the house. Unsure of where they led, Dotty stared upwards into the dark. The heavy wooden door at the top of the steps was ajar, just a little, letting through a chink of light.

Drawn to what might be beyond the darkness of the stairwell, Dotty started to climb, gingerly at first. The steps were old and narrow and creaked under her tread, but Dotty was sure-footed and could easily navigate them. Gaining confidence she ran up the last few steps and threw open the door to see what the chink of light might uncover. As she alighted on the top step she found herself in a beautiful big room: the one room in the house that she had most wanted to find. It was her mother's playroom: 'Mam's Playroom'.

The light, airy playroom was big enough for ten children to play in with a large blackboard, a rocking chair, and box upon box of toys. There was a wooden cuckoo clock on the playroom wall, sitting to one side of a huge window through which the light poured into the room. Dotty noticed that the stained glass in the window panes depicted nursery rhyme characters and realised that the room must have been designed as a playroom.

There was Little Jack Horner holding up a plum, Little Miss Muffet with the spider and Mary and her little lamb. The stained glass threw droplets of coloured light into the room and it sat on the walls like brightly coloured candies sparkling in the sunshine. Dotty was reminded of her mum's favourite sweets: boxes of jellies called Newbury Fruits that she had always bought at Christmas. As a small child she had always thought the jellies looked like sparkly jewels. With their sweet, sticky liquid centres, such a surprise to find in a jelly, the sweets seemed to have a secretive air of decadence about them not found in any other confection, even chocolate.

Dotty watched the light play on the walls for a moment, before turning to take in the contents of the room. The wallpaper was clearly old, cream with a pretty small print on it, again obviously designed for a child's room. There were little black cats and horseshoes and clover leaves and little round brushes. It was enchanting. Even though, as with the downstairs rooms, there were dust sheets over many of the items in the playroom, Dotty saw perfection from the word go. She toured the room, pulling off the dust sheets one by one: each revealing a new treasure. There was a rocking horse; a painting easel; and a doll's house as intricate in design and as detailed as the house she stood in. Dotty peered through one of the windows and saw that the furniture mirrored that of the Calendar House too.

Dotty couldn't believe that this was the same room that her mum had played in as a little girl (mind you, she couldn't believe her mum hadn't told her she grew up in a mansion in Yorkshire either, for that matter). She picked up one toy after another, touching them, handling them, holding them, and breathing in their scent. The room had the smell of her mother about it. Dotty even fancied she could catch a whiff of her perfume, although of course her mum would never have worn perfume as a child. Dotty tried to imagine her mother as an infant, playing happily in the room the very fabric of which seemed to contain her essence.

"Oh, Mam, I miss you so much!" Dotty cried to the un-answering walls. It was then that the tears began to flow. If only her mother was here with Dotty now; in this room in which she felt so tangibly close. Dotty absent-mindedly gathered up a doll to her chest, cradling it as she wept.

For a moment she was angry with her great uncle. Tears stung in her eyes and smarted on her cheeks. How could he leave her so alone and so suddenly? Dotty rocked the doll, calming herself in doing so, and started to breathe more easily. She knew in truth that, despite his absence, Great Uncle Winchester had gone to a lot of effort to make her feel welcome on her arrival at the big house, and that there was nothing malicious about his sudden departure. The fact remained however that, for all its beauty, her lovely bedroom overlooking the garden, with its grand four poster bed, and this magnificent playroom that reminded her so much of her mother, lacked the one thing she really needed at the moment: a friend. Being sat alone in this vast and beautiful playroom: a room that should be filled with laughter and not tears - just seemed to highlight how alone Dotty really was in this grand old house. All the toys and games somehow just made her feel all the more alone, knowing she had no-one to share them with.

Dotty's thoughts were interrupted by a noise that made her almost jump out of her skin. It was the chimneys again: *scraaaatchh!* She scanned the room for its fireplace as she hadn't noticed one when she walked in. Her eyes came to rest on an old cast iron range with a little kettle sitting on top of it, quite dainty in comparison to the great open hearths in the downstairs rooms. Like all the other fireplaces in the house, though, it was beautifully decorated, with fishing boats and leaping fish, and at the bottom little children swimming under the water.

The chimney came alive again with its *scritch-scratch* and then a *ker-plunk*! Soot billowed out of the range's small cast iron hatch. Something had fallen down the chimney. Dropping the doll, Dotty leaped up to investigate, tears forgotten.

The little door was quite heavy but Dotty managed to prize it open, immediately wishing she hadn't because a huge amount of soot poured from the open door as she did so. Dirty black clouds billowed around the room. If only she hadn't removed all those dust covers, Dotty thought. Waiting for the dirt to settle, she peered inside the grate but she couldn't see anything of interest. She made to close the door again but she was unable because the opening was now clogged up with soot. There was nothing for it but to clear the dirt away. She would have to ask Gobby for a dustpan and brush later.

Dotty began to scrape with her hands, her nails immediately blackening with the grime. At first there was nothing but soot, but then she saw a fragment of cloth. She pulled at it, dislodging more dirt and ash from the fire as she did so. With a bit more tugging and a lot more mess, Dotty managed to wrench the cloth free. She surveyed it carefully. The cloth, it appeared, was actually quite fine linen underneath all that dirt, and at once she saw that it was a handkerchief, once white in colour, despite its now very black appearance. Dotty examined the little handkerchief parcel, noting the tattered lace around it edges. It would have been quite a pretty thing before it had been given its current use.

Gently, Dotty unwound the folded cloth from around its long hidden contents. She gasped at the beauty of what lay inside. It was a gold locket on a chain, the front inlaid with pearls in an intricate design. There seemed to be no way of opening the locket, though. Turning it over in her hand Dotty discovered that there was instead a photograph inlaid into the back of the gold case, covered in glass. The handkerchief had kept the locket quite clean, or so she had thought, but no, some soot must have found its way beneath the glass, because the picture appeared quite dirty.

Dotty examined the photograph more closely. Hang on a minute! It wasn't dirt on the photograph at all: the face of the young man in the picture was all dirty with soot! Dotty knew from Gobby that her family had made their fortune from the coal mining industry but she was sure they would have had the wherewithal to wash before having their photographs taken. Her mum was always frantic before school photograph day, making Dotty scrub her face until it hurt and brushing her tangled mane of reddish-brown hair to within an inch of its life. She wondered what her mum would have made of it all, or whether she had known anything about it.

Instinctually Dotty put the locket around her neck for safekeeping. Then, glancing down at the handkerchief that had been its keeper, her heart skipped a beat. In the middle of the small square of linen, perfectly preserved and clean from where the locket had lain, was a delicately embroidered letter 'G'. Dotty could barely breathe. Her mother's name had been Gwen. Perhaps the locket belonged to her. But why would she hide such a thing and why did she never return to claim it? Could her mother have forgotten it was there? Perhaps Great Uncle Winchester would know something of it.

Tucking the locket under her now very grubby nightie, she resolved to ask him on his return from London.

Jackdaws

Chapter 5

Meeting Geoff

In which Dotty makes a new friend

Dotty never got a chance to tidy up the mess in Mam's Playroom: as soon as Gobby saw her, she frog-marched Dotty straight upstairs to the bathroom and into the tub.

"My goodness, girl! How on earth did you get into this state? Didn't I tell you not to go messing about near fireplaces?" Gobby was beside herself. "What on earth were you doing poking around in the chimney anyway?"

Dotty sat in the bath tub, the bubbles turned grey from the sooty residue she had deposited into it. She was beyond making any form of protestation and sat in silence, suitably abashed. She had omitted from her explanations her discovery of her mother's locket (if, indeed, it was hers). She wasn't quite sure why she had done this. It certainly might have reduced the scolding from the irate cook, but something told her this was best kept a secret, at least until she had spoken to Great Uncle Winchester.

"When you ran off earlier I was worried and now I can see for good reason," continued Gobby crossly, scrubbing furiously at Dotty with a loofah. "You obviously need someone to keep a closer eye on you to see you don't get yourself into any trouble." Abandoning the sponge Gobby picked up a bottle of shampoo and poured it liberally over Dotty's matted and now wet mane of hair. "I told Mr Winchester it would come to no good, leaving a young girl cooped up all day in this big old house without company." She massaged the soap into Dotty's head with vigour. "Still, I suppose that's why he left Geoff: to guide you away from mischief."

Dotty's ears pricked up. "Who's Geoff?" Dotty was intrigued. Perhaps this was the friend Great Uncle Winchester had wanted to introduce her to before his sudden departure.

"Aha, I thought you mustn't have read the whole of Mr Winchester's letter when you took off so," remarked the cook. "It did seem strange you leaving without even stopping to say 'hello'." Gobby poured a jug of water over Dotty's head, rinsing off the soap and another dose of soot in a river of grey foam.

Chapter 5

"Anyway, I left your great uncle's letter on your bedside table, so you can read it when you've finished dressing. And then I suggest you come down and meet him. He's starting to look terribly bored and I'm sure he'd benefit a dose of fresh air, as would you, young lady." Gobby thrust an oversized and impossibly fluffy white towel at Dotty.

"What? You mean he's still here?" Without stopping for answers Dotty leapt out of the tub and grabbed the towel from the waiting cook, rubbing and scrubbing herself dry as she ran with it to her bedroom.

"I'll be getting back to my macaroons then, shall I?" Gobby shouted after Dotty's fleeing form. "I'll tell Geoff you're on your way."

Dotty was too preoccupied with the contents of Great Uncle Winchester's letter to reply. Picking it up from the bedside table where it lay neatly folded, Dotty opened the letter and scanned to the end. There was a post script at the bottom that she hadn't noticed when she was scanning it before. It read:

> P.s. ... Please would you look after my old pal Geoff whilst I am away? I'm sure he would welcome the company in my absence.
>
> W x

Whoever could it be? Dotty pulled on jeans and a jumper and, donning her roller-blades for speed, raced down the corridor. Stairs are never easy to navigate with wheels but Dotty managed without too much bother (or, in any event, without accident) and arrived unscathed in the kitchen. Gobby had taken up her usual post at the kitchen table and was tutting over a batch of macaroons, clearly burnt.

"Well," she said with finality. "The only thing these are good for now is Geoff."

Dotty eyed Gobby with surprise. Usually the cook was extremely house-proud when it came to her baking and she certainly wouldn't dream of giving spoiled confection of any description to a house guest. She wondered if Gobby didn't like Geoff, for some reason. Or maybe it was just that Dotty's adventure in the chimney had put the usually jovial cook in just about the worst mood ever; she certainly did seem to have a thing against chimneys.

"Erm...where might I find Geoff, Mrs Gobbins?" Dotty ventured, not keen to cause more upset, whether she or Geoff himself was the source of it.

"He's in the boot room dear, just by the back door to the left of the laundry. I don't like him in the kitchen – he always steals my pastries." Gobby turned her nose up in disgust at the thought of it.

Wow, Gobby really doesn't like this person, thought Dotty. *But why ever not?*

As Dotty turned to go, Gobby unceremoniously scraped the over-cooked macaroons into a Tupperware and handed it to her. "And don't forget these," she said. Dotty did as she was told, but made a mental note to ditch them at the first opportunity. She wasn't particularly *au fait* with the social niceties of country house living but even Dotty's, to date, modest upbringing told her that it would be difficult not to take offence at the burnt offering that had been provided.

Negotiating a maze of service rooms Dotty made her way towards the back door. She skated past a large pantry, the laundry and a downstairs cloakroom obviously reserved for staff use in the days before there was only a handful of staff at the grand house. Finally, she came to the boot room, immediately to the left of the back door, just as Gobby had described. Opening the door, Dotty peered inside, but she couldn't see anyone there. She heaved a sigh of disappointment. Perhaps Geoff had got fed up with waiting for her and had left.

Dotty slumped down on a low bench that ran the length of the room, in amidst piles of boots and shoes; her back leaning against a row of waxed and tweed jackets of various lengths and descriptions, and in varying states of cleanliness. Plonking the Tupperware down beside her, she contemplated what to do with the rest of her already eventful day. Suddenly Dotty heard a snuffling sound. It seemed to be coming from beneath the bench. What was it with this house and its strange noises?

The sniffing stopped. Forgetting the macaroons, Dotty stood up to go, stretching as she did so. More sniffs followed, and then a 'thwop' as the forgotten Tupperware fell to the floor. She turned. The broken macaroons were scattered across the floor, but still she could see nobody in the room. Nervous now, Dotty knelt awkwardly in her skates and started to clear up the mess it seemed she had created for the second time that day. Reaching under the bench for a stray macaroon, she felt a warm breath on her hand. Slowly she pulled the macaroon out from under the bench. The breath followed, as did a big brown velvety nose. It was a dog.

Squeezing himself out from under the bench, the rather portly brown and white spaniel looked at Dotty with a doleful 'feed me' expression. Dotty obliged, feeding the dog one of the spoiled macaroons. She giggled as he licked every last crumb of broken macaroon from her hand and, when he had finished, gave him a little rub on the head.

"Now what's your name, boy?" Dotty asked the spaniel, feeling for his collar beneath his shaggy coat. Seeking out the circle of leather in amongst the folds of his neck, she followed it around with her fingers until she found the small disc of metal that served as his name plate. The writing on it was tiny and the script very old fashioned, but Dotty could just make it out.

"Of course," she said, grinning. "I should have known. Hello Geoff."

Geoff and Dotty's friendship was quickly cemented with the provision of a few more burnt macaroons and over the days that followed the pair soon became inseparable. Where Dotty went, Geoff went; and where Geoff went, there followed Dotty. As a result, an otherwise dull week waiting for Great Uncle Winchester's return passed quite pleasantly, Dotty spending much of her time either rummaging about in the garden with Geoff or hanging around the kitchens seeing what Gobby was up to.

Dotty soon learned that Geoff was not altogether welcome in the kitchen however, with Gobby shrieking "Get that scrounging mongrel out of here!" whenever she caught a glimpse of him. Dotty thought this quite unfair: whilst opportunistic he might be, a mongrel he most certainly was not. Dotty was quite sure he was a pedigree. There were even agility trials rosettes from Geoff's younger days hung up in the downstairs cloakroom, although looking at his rotund silhouette Dotty found it hard to picture a time when the spaniel had been agile enough to climb over anything, let alone jump over it.

In the house, the scritch-scratching of the chimneys continued, much to Dotty's annoyance. The garden was a safe haven though, and the pair spent many a long hour exploring the grounds. Whilst Geoff dug to retrieve some long-forgotten bone from the frost covered earth Dotty delighted in the discovery of some new dew-laden nook or hidden dell or exchanged pleasantries with the resident gardener-cum-odd job man, Kenneth Diswold, known to his friends as Kenny.

"Good morning, Kenny!" Dotty would call out, whenever she saw him, and Kenny would nod in greeting, rubbing his gloved hands together against the bite of the winter cold. There was always plenty to keep him busy, even in the winter season when the plants and trees slumbered their way to the spring. Kenny was a man of few words, but Dotty soon learned that he carried quietly about him a wealth of knowledge about the house and its gardens, planted by his great grandfather and tended by three generations of Diswolds since then.

If plied with a cup of tea, strong with two sugars, Kenny could be persuaded to stop his toil for a moment or two and warm his hands against the earthenware mug, answering a brief question or two about the garden: the name of a bird or a plant, or where the best spots in the garden were to catch the fleeting morning sun, or how to make the best den out of fallen twigs and branches, at least before Kenny tidied them away.

When not with Geoff (usually when he was being fed: a duty carried out by Kenny as Gobby flatly refused the task), Dotty often returned to Mam's Playroom, to her surprise finding that she really rather liked to be there on her own. Just being in the playroom Dotty somehow fancied that her dear departed mother was with her, their souls connected in this very special place of her mum's childhood, that had now become her own. Alone there Dotty would talk and talk to the pretty wallpaper that her mum had once gazed upon, all the while turning over in her hands the locket with the strange picture, there hoping to discover its secrets.

Dotty also liked to play with the vast array of toys the room contained, each visit producing some new discovery: an old teddy; a jar of brightly coloured marbles; a dainty china tea set. Dotty's favourite thing was the doll's house, however, and she returned to it again and again. She found it fascinating that the house resembled in every detail the Calendar House in which she now resided, and she spent hours studying its features, its layout and its contents. Dotty wanted to know everything about it.

But there were discrepancies: inconsistencies that were difficult to ignore. This was a Calendar house, and as such should have 365 windows, but the doll's house had only 364. Dotty counted the windows and then counted again, but she always came to the same number. The house was missing a window. With so many windows in the house it was an easy mistake for the maker of the model to make, reasoned Dotty. It was just that they had been so particular in every other detail it seemed strange that they should make such an error.

And there was something else that was strange about the Doll's house too. The Calendar House in miniature was square in shape. This was entirely faithful to its life-sized counterpart, as Dotty's tour of the gardens had evidenced; but the doll's house had a courtyard in the middle: something which Dotty was sure the Calendar house did not. Why then would the maker of this fancy model have introduced such a feature, she wondered?

Yet more strangely, the courtyard contained a street scene, busy with market stalls and all manner of figures carrying about their daily business, many of the characters carrying chimney brooms. This again was odd, particularly in light of the fact that the courtyard appeared to have no entrance or exit, nor indeed any method of access to or from the world beyond the house.

How on earth, then, did these good people of the doll's house go to their homes at the end of a busy market day? It must simply be the fancy of the toymaker, Dotty concluded. Any courtyard that did exist at the Calendar House (and Dotty was aware of none) would have been empty, and not bristling full of a busy days' work in the town.

Over the next few days the noises in the chimneys continued. *Scritch, scratch, scritchety-scratch.*

Dotty was sure it wasn't jackdaws, as Gobby had said. Apart from anything else the noises didn't appear like the random scratching of a bird. They were odd noises. Dotty would even have sworn on one occasion she heard the distinct whistling of a tune, something she was sure even the most musical of songbirds could not achieve with that degree of accuracy. The whole thing was quite unsettling. In fact, Dotty thought it was starting to get a bit creepy.

Dotty's feelings were not helped by the fact that Geoff could hear the noises too. Whilst, on one level, it was good for Dotty to know they were not a figment of her nine and a half year old imagination, Geoff's reaction to the noises was far from reassuring. Rather than barking at them and sniffing and scraping at the hearth, as one might expect of a hunting dog, Geoff took to hiding from the noise.

And yet more worryingly, whereas Chip and Pin had been eager in the winter weather to sit as close to the fire as possible, roasting themselves until they could bear the heat no longer and then retiring, panting, to a more congenial spot by the sofa, Geoff seemed to go out of his way to put as much distance between himself and the fire as he could. Indeed his preferred tack seemed to be to take up residence in the far corner of the room by the door, thereby acting as a quite effective draft excluder. This, Dotty was sure, was not normal, especially in this cold Yorkshire weather they were having.

Great Uncle Winchester had now been away for a whole week and Christmas was fast approaching. The morning was fine and crisp, and Dotty was down in the formal garden kicking up dead leaves in what Dotty liked to call 'The Maze', although she was reliably told by Kenny that it was a not a maze, but a faithful replica of an Elizabethan knot garden, planted by Kenny's father. "You see there are no dead ends with a knot garden. The shapes just make a pretty pattern." He informed her. Whatever it was, Dotty liked it for her own reasons. From the maze there was a really great view of the house and Dotty took some time to look up at it.

As well as a lot of windows the house had a huge number of chimneys, and Dotty studied them as Geoff sniffed around in the shrubbery. Gazing up at the plethora of chimney stacks, something struck Dotty as not being quite right. Now what was it? Dotty blanched as the realisation struck her: there were no bird nests! If Gobby was right and it had been jackdaws nesting on top of the chimney pots that were making the noise that carried down the chimneys, where on earth were their nests? All of a sudden, Dotty felt more than a little scared.

As she stood, rooted to the spot in alarm, Kenny sidled up to Dotty, scratching at the dead leaves with an oversized rake. Dotty jumped and let out a squeal.

"Sorry, Dotty," said the gardener. "Did I frighten you there? Why, child, you are pale. Are you quite alright?"

"Mrs Gobbins said there were jackdaws nesting in the chimneys, but I can't see any nests." Dotty stammered.

"Jackdaws, you say?" Kenneth paused, choosing his words. "The bane of my life are jackdaws. Always pecking at my seedlings. They're not welcome here," he scowled.

"Sure we do get them over in the vegetable garden, but they don't nest on the chimneys: they can't." Kenneth squinted up at the vast roof of Calendar House and pointed: "can you spot those metal cages up on top of the chimney pots Dotty?' They are chimney cowls. Put there to prevent birds from nesting on the chimney stacks. The jackdaws couldn't nest there even if they wanted to. See?"

"But I heard them whistling," countered Dotty. "Whistling a tune."

"Whistling, eh?" said the old man, leaning heavily on his rake. "Well they's clever birds, them jackdaws, that's for sure. I suppose there could be truth in that, girl," he mused. "But nesting on them there chimneys, they most definitely are not. Chimney cowls, see?" And with that Kenny turned away and continued with his raking.

That night the noises were worse than ever. It was blustery high on the hill where the Calendar House stood and the wind howled around the walls and rattled the window panes. This, interspersed with the scritchings and scratchings of the chimney, was almost more than Dotty could bear. She clung to the covers, bedspread pulled tightly up to her chin and the bed curtains firmly closed against the whining and scratching beyond. To her it felt as if a great animal was prowling around her, trying to gain entrance to her sanctuary.

Suddenly, the scrapings of the chimney became more frantic, drowning out the pitiful cries of the wind. *Scritch-scratch, scrape scraaATCCH!* Something was falling: tumbling and falling down the chimney at great speed, and that something was very large. Could it really be a great, huge jackdaw? Dotty listened, terrified; too scared to take a breath, as the noise and its bearer hurtled towards the room.

Finally, with an almighty THUD it landed, amid a great flapping and coughing, and Dotty smelled the faint odour of soot emanating through the thick damask of the drapes.

There was nothing for it, Dotty had to find out what it was that had come down the chimney and invaded her bedroom. Leaning gingerly towards the bed curtains her trembling hand found their joining. Slowly she reached around with her hand, snapping on the bedside lamp.

Chapter 5

Armed with a little light, she slowly drew back the drape.

And there on the hearth she saw it, standing in the lamplight, coughing and stamping and dusting itself off: the largest jackdaw Dotty had ever seen.

Except it wasn't a jackdaw at all.

It was a boy.

Meeting Geoff

Chapter 6

The Boy in the Chimney

In which Dotty discovers there are more than jackdaws in the chimneys

Dotty gaped. She felt she should scream but her mouth had gone dry and no sound would come out. Instead she stood, mouth open, shrieking mentally for good measure.

The boy did indeed resemble a jackdaw, or a sooty sparrow, at least. He was about Dotty's height but clearly small for his age. Dotty would have guessed he was about eleven or twelve. He was as skinny as a rake, his clothes all tattered and patched; all knees and elbows and hair like straw. His hair was straw-coloured too Dotty would have guessed although it was difficult to tell because, despite his great show of dusting himself off, the boy was absolutely filthy. He was also barefoot, she noticed.

"Wh..wh..what…? Where on earth…? Who…? Who are you?" spluttered Dotty.

"As for the *who*: Pip's the name," replied the boy, "It's short for Peregrine," he said. "But it's too much of a mouthful for most people, so everyone just calls me Pip." The boy took a low bow. "At your service, Miss," he grinned.

Dotty continued to gape.

"As for the *where:*" the boy continued, "I came down your chimney. A fact that, begging your pardon, Miss, I would have thought quite obvious and, as for the *what*: well, I'm an apprentisweep, aren't I?" The boy gesticulated, waving about a chimney brush in his right hand to demonstrate his trade. Dotty hadn't noticed he was carrying anything before.

She stared in disbelief, rubbing her eyes as if to chase away a dream. The dirty sparrow of a boy remained, however, as clear as day and as life-like as ever.

"A *prenty*-what?" Dotty blinked and then double-blinked; struggling to focus her mind as well as her eyes.

"An AP-PRENT-I-SWEEP," repeated Pip slowly and rather more loudly this time. "You know: a chimney sweep; a climbing boy; apprentice to the Master Sweep?" he said looking at her first hopefully, but then somewhat dubiously.

Chapter 6

Finding her voice at last, Dotty retorted "I'm sure I have no idea what you are talking about. And anyway, that still doesn't explain what you are doing lurking in my chimney and bursting into my bedroom like that, scaring me half to death." Dotty spoke with some indignation, hands on hips, as her confidence momentarily returned to her.

The boy seemed as taken aback by Dotty's outburst as she had been by his dramatic entrance into her bedroom. The pair eyed each other for a second before the boy spoke again.

"Look," he explained. "I'm sorry to have startled you, Miss. But it's just that I would have thought they'd have told you about us, that's all."

"Who are they? Who are *us*?! You mean there are MORE of you?" Suddenly Dotty was not so in control; she was beginning to feel a bit faint.

"But of course there are more of us sweeps and well, Gwennie of course: your mother."

Dotty reeled. The room started to spin. She couldn't take it all in.

"Why don't you and me start again?" offered the boy. "I'm Pip." He offered Dotty his blackened hand.

Dotty staggered backwards, scrabbling for the safety of her bed, hoping to shut the sooty vision out with her curtains. Her mother? No, it couldn't be.

"I don't believe you!" cried Dotty. "Go away, go *away!*" Dotty scrambled back onto her mattress, snatching the heavy curtains closed behind her, shutting the boy out. The strange boy followed, stopping short of the bed and talking through the curtains.

"Well I'm so very sorry, Miss!" shouted Pip through the brocade, his voice now muffled. "I didn't realise you was so 'igh and mighty. Your mother never was." The boy continued "I 'appened upon your room in search of the Calendar House Key, but obviously it 'aint 'ere so I shall be off and a good day to you." And with that the boy marched back to the fireplace, held his broom aloft: arm straight up as if he was holding a large sooty umbrella, and disappeared, *poof!* back up the chimney.

Sensing him gone, Dotty poked her head out through the heavy drapes once more. With just her face showing she scoured the room for any sign of him. Only the boy's dirty footprints gave away any indication that he had been there at all.

Dotty felt a flood of relief followed by a sudden sense of disappointment. Who was this boy: this Pip character? Had he really known her mother? Were there really others like him? And what was this key he was looking for: the Calendar House Key? Dotty had so many questions and now no-one to answer them. She edged her way nervously towards the open fireplace. Perhaps he was still up the chimney. After all, he couldn't have crawled away that quickly. "Hello?" she called. "Hello Pip?"

Nothing.

Taking a deep breath Dotty put one foot into the fireplace. She squeezed her eyes shut, fearful that she too might go flying up the chimney. Nothing happened. She brought the other foot in and stood up straight, all the while looking up. Dotty could still hear the howl of the wind and the dripping of raindrops into the chimney shaft, but the chimney was otherwise empty and she could see nothing above it: not even the sky. It was just a dark void that went up and up into the blackness.

Dotty called up the chimney. "Pip, I'm sorry," she faltered. "Please come back." But nothing happened. No dirty raggedy boy appeared in the chimney beside her, nor did Pip offer any reply.

Feeling rather stupid and with a small sigh, Dotty climbed out of the fireplace and dusted herself down. She had soot on her nightdress. Gobby would have something to say about that, she was sure.

"Perhaps I'm going crazy," Dotty said to herself. "That's it. I'm going crazy and seeing things which aren't there. After all, I'm talking to myself so I must be at least half crazy. Seeing people in the chimney must be the next step."

And with that, Dotty climbed back into her bed and bade herself a weary good night, her tired eyes awash with visions of keys and jackdaws and dirty little boys, the strange pattern on the heavy damask swimming around her.

Dotty awoke with a start the next morning, the recollection of the night's happenings still crowding her tired brain. Poking her head out from the bed curtains, she instantly saw the dirty footmarks around the hearth. So it wasn't just a dream, she thought. This boy, Pip, really did exist. But did he really know her mother as he had claimed? As Dotty slid herself down from the high feather mattress, feet seeking out her slippers before her eyes found them, she once again caught a glance of the unusual pattern on the heavy bed curtain. Her eyes widened. Suddenly everything seemed to come into focus. Why ever hadn't she seen it before? The miniature characters that danced across the drapes were tiny sweeps!

It was what Dotty's dad would have called a *Eureka!* moment. All the strange little details Dotty had noticed around the house, they were all connected; connected to the world of sweeps! There was no other explanation for it: Dotty's mum must have known about the boy in the chimney all along. Pip was telling the truth!

"Pip!" Dotty raced to the fireplace, shoving her head up into the darkness. She yelled again with all her might: "*PIIPPPPP!*" Desperate to find the little sweep she called up into the darkness again and again, but to no avail. Pip wasn't there.

Oh why, oh why wasn't he there when she needed him?

In search of more answers to the unravelling mystery, Dotty ran to Mam's Playroom, tearing along the corridor and up the little wooden staircase. In her hurried efforts to get to the doll's house she knocked over the fine dappled grey rocking horse and it clattered on the floor. But Dotty's attention was elsewhere. She stood over the doll's house, breathless, peering down into its strange central courtyard: the courtyard containing the busy street scene. It was a crowded scene, Dotty remembered, but yes, there it was again, quite unmistakably: sweeps. The street was filled with chimney sweeps! Dotty stared at the tiny little figures, perfect in every detail, with their bare feet and dirty faces, and their circular chimney brushes. There could now be no question as to whether her mum knew about the sweeps; the only question that remained was whether she had been the only one in the Calendar House to know about it, or whether the whole household knew. Dotty was sure that Pip would be able to tell her. But Pip was nowhere to be found.

It occurred to Dotty that if only she could find her way into the courtyard she would perhaps be in with a chance of finding him, or at least in with a chance of discovering some of the answers to her questions. She scoured the model of the Calendar House in vain, pausing over every detail, every brick: the answer must lie here somewhere. And then she saw it. There in the courtyard, under cover of a brightly coloured awning was a window; a solitary window facing the street: the only window from which the courtyard could be seen from the House. Now if only Dotty could find the room to which that window belonged, she could perhaps access the courtyard and find Pip.

Dotty knelt down on the floor and, turning the doll's house around, she peered into the darkness of the ground floor rooms to discover which one it could be. She drew in a sharp breath: the room was an office. But it wasn't just any office, not just another one of the many and varied service rooms that benefited the house; this was the very finest of offices. Dotty almost didn't recognise it as the room she had visited because of the absence of the many piles of books that lay strewn around the floor in its life-sized twin; but there was no mistaking it: it was Great Uncle Winchester's study.

Dotty leapt up from the floor. That meant Great Uncle Winchester could see all the comings and goings of the courtyard and its daily business from his study window. He must know about the presence of the sweeps too! It was time to unearth the next piece of the puzzle. Hurtling down the little wooden stairs, she tripped on the last but one and sprawling across the corridor, grazing her knee. Nothing serious though.

Picking herself up, Dotty tore down the corridor, on and on, until she came to her great uncle's study: the only door on the left hand side of the corridor. The study door was closed. She rattled the great brass knob but without luck, the door was locked.

Just then she felt a chill down her spine; and the great sense of unease that came with the knowledge of a malevolent presence behind her. It was Strake.

"Miss Parsons. As you are aware, Mr. Winchester is not yet returned from his trip to London. Is there anything I can help you with?" Strake gave his approximation of a smile that looked more like a sneer.

"Er, no thank you." Dotty paused. "Well, I was wondering if I might be able to take a look in his study?" she faltered. "I left something in there and I need it now."

"I'm afraid that won't be possible, Miss Parsons." Strake was clearly enjoying the opportunity to say no to her. "Mr. Winchester's office is full of confidential papers and strictly out of bounds to third parties…with the exception of myself, of course." Strake sneered: a definite sneer this time.

"Okay, well thanks," Dotty managed, before turning on her heel and, realising she was still in her nightie, made her way back to her bedroom to dress.

Never one to be deterred by a setback, as Dotty walked back up the long corridor, she resolved to make a plan to get into the study. After all, a simple plan was all she needed: it was just that she didn't have one right now; that was all. If only Pip was there to help her; she was sure that he would be able to.

Over the next few days Dotty often called up to Pip in the darkness, but there came no response. Tiring of her fruitless pursuit she began to think that the boy had been the product of her over-active imagination after all. Just a strange and vivid dream cobbling together all the things that had happened since her arrival at the house and culminating in an uncannily life-like vision of a small boy. Only Dotty couldn't quite believe this, though she tried to tell herself it was the case. For no matter how hard she tried she couldn't eradicate the sooty footprints from the fireside rug.

The weather had been inclement ever since the night of Pip's appearance, which made walks in the gardens distinctly less appealing. Much to Geoff's disgust, Dotty resorted to dividing her time between Mam's Playroom and the pretty drawing room on the ground floor: Dotty's Bird Room. Dotty liked to go there to read, curling herself up by the fireplace, log fire roaring, with its life-like figures embracing around it; or sitting in the window seat with its view of the garden out onto the boating lake beyond.

The gardens were still pretty to look at, even when they were too wet and dreary to play out in; and the lake itself was vast. In the tempestuous weather it seemed to Dotty like a small enclosed sea, full of tides and waves caused by the wind howling across its surface.

It was a drizzly afternoon and Dotty was sitting by the fire, Geoff taking up his usual position in the far side of the room by the door, as if preparing for a quick get-away. Suddenly with a great whoosh! A big clod of soot fell down into the fireplace, drowning the flames and putting out the fire.

As Dotty jumped to her feet, the eerie *scritch-scratch* started in the chimney. There followed a rolling and a tumbling and out of the fireplace erupted the familiar form of an exceptionally sooty small boy. It was Pip.

"Good afternoon, Miss. And how are you this fine wet day?" Pip grinned his sooty smile in greeting.

Dotty pouted in complaint, "Oh Pip, where have you been? I've been looking for you everywhere, or in every chimney at least."

"Sorry, Miss Dorothy, but, as I tried to explain to you the other day, I've been very busy. I'm on an important mission, you know. Top secret and of the utmost importance it is. A matter of life and death!"

Pip puffed out his chest, clearly proud of having been given such a responsible task.

"It's Dorothea," corrected Dotty, "but my friends call me Dotty."

"Okay, Miss Dotty it is then." Pip smiled his best smile at her. "I have to say I'm a little surprised you're so pleased to see me, although I'm delighted, of course. I wasn't altogether sure after our last meeting that you ever wanted to lay eyes on me again, you took on so."

Dotty smiled back, sheepishly. "I'm sorry, Pip, but you did give me a fright you know, tumbling down my chimney like that in the middle of the night."

"That's quite alright, Miss Dotty," said Pip. "I knew you didn't have knowledge of us sweeps when you refused to shake my hand. There's not many folks what would say no to a sweeps handshake, you know; even that of a young sweep such as myself."

"Why ever not?" Dotty questioned. "No offence but I would have thought there wouldn't be many people who *would* want to shake your hand, dirty as it is."

"None taken." replied the boy. "But that's my point, ain't it? No-one's ever told you about the luck a sweep carries in his hand, have they, Miss Dotty? It rubs off, you know." Pip explained, chest swelling again. Clearly he was very proud of his trade.

"Haven't you ever heard the saying? If a sweep shakes hands with you, you have good luck for the rest of the day?" His question was rhetorical, and he continued. "Blowing a person a kiss works too, but you are only allowed to do that once you are fourteen, and as I am only twelve, I can't do that yet." He frowned with impatience at the thought.

"I can't say I have heard," remarked Dotty, "but it all sounds like nonsense to me."

"Well you may say, Miss," Pip countered, "well you may say. But you wait until it happens to you. Then you'll believe me, as sure as eggs is eggs."

"Well we'll just have to see, won't we?" Dotty replied. "But enough of that anyway. I have a million questions to ask you, and I want answers before you go disappearing off again back up that chimney!"

"Okay, okay, Little Miss Impatient. Go on, I'm all ears. What do you want to know?" Pip settled himself down cross-legged on the fireside rug and leant forwards with an expression of deep concentration.

"Well what I *really* want to know is all about my mum," said Dotty. "But it sounds to me like you've got urgent business on your hands, so perhaps you should tell me all about that first. What is this Calendar House Key you're looking for? Perhaps I can help you find it."

The Boy in the Chimney

Chapter 7

The Calendar House Key

In which Dotty discovers the true nature of her mother's locket

"Well, Miss Dotty," said Pip, taking a deep breath and settling down into his story. "There's quite a lot to tell, you know."

"That's alright, Pip," Dotty encouraged. "It's not like I've got anything else to do, is it?" She smiled winningly, urging him to indulge her.

"Okay then," said the boy. "As you ask so nicely. It all started a long time ago, in the early days of the sweeps. The sweeps and the ordinary folk lived quite happily side by side at that time, without any thought to their differences. The ordinary folk saw us sweeps as the guardians of the fireside, and they would call upon us to clean and keep their chimneys safe. Climbing boys like myself, the so-called *apprentisweeps*, were apprenticed to the master sweeps under the watchful eye of the Sweeps' Council, learning the art of sweeping and the proper and safe use of sweeps' magick for the task. And a vital part of this magick was the art of chimney hopping: travelling through the chimneys from place to place, and from chimney to chimney."

"Now in those carefree days many sweeps were in the habit of giving a little bit of sweeps' magick to the ordinary folk, in the form of 'chimney keys'. These keys possessed the power to allow the ordinary folk to chimney hop, just like the sweeps could, both from house to house and in and out of the world of the sweeps. The ordinary folk used the keys for calling on the sweeps, and for the pure pleasure of chimney hopping too."

"Wow that sounds amazing!" Dotty exclaimed. "But how did the keys work?"

"Oh, it was simple," explained Pip. "Just a little bit of Sweeps' magick, wrapped up in a trinket: a piece of jewellery, usually."

"I see. But how was that done?" quizzed Dotty, not at all clear. "It seems to me quite a difficult thing, to 'catch' a piece of magick!"

Pip sighed, just a little impatiently. "A chimney key is easy enough to make," he described. "All you have to do is to capture a kiss blown by a sweep and the magick from that kiss allows you to travel through the chimneys." Pip paused for effect. "The tricky part is keeping the kiss safe. You need to trap it in something sturdy that you can carry with you, like a ring or a pendant, for example. Anything like that really."

"Wow! that is clever," Dotty marvelled.

"Not really," shrugged Pip. "Anyway: getting back to the story. Some people didn't like the sweeps giving away their secrets so freely. You ordinary folk aren't as trusting as we sweeps were back then. The ordinary folk were jealous of the sweeps' magick and they were frightened of it, being suspicious of what they couldn't understand.

Before we knew it, rumours had begun to spread between the ordinary folk that sweeps were using their magick to enter the homes of the ordinary folk uninvited and there cause all manner of mischief. It was a story that could never have been further from the truth, of course, Miss Dotty."

"Yes, of course, Pip," Dotty nodded vigorously in assent.

"Quite right, Miss Dotty; quite right. And so the ordinary folk, afraid of what we sweeps might do, started turning their backs on the old ways, planning in secret to have their chimneys cleaned without the use of sweeps' magick."

"These were dark days indeed, Miss. To make matters worse, a group of rogue sweeps saw a profit in the situation. They started offering chimney sweeping services to the ordinary folk with the promise that no magick would be used. The Sweeps' Council was furious. They tried to stop the rogue sweeps of course, but it was no use."

"But was that really so bad?" asked Dotty. "Do you really need magic to sweep a chimney?"

"Why yes, of course," Pip retorted. "You see this is the thing you ordinary folk don't understand. Chimney work without the use of sweeps' magick is awful dangerous, Miss Dotty: nothing short of madness, really. The poor climbing boys and girls that worked under the rogue sweeps, not properly apprenticed or taught the use of magick, suffered terrible injuries and hardships, and sometimes worse. We tried to look out for them of course, following them up the chimneys whenever we got wind of an unauthorised sweeping…"

Pip hung his head. "Oh, Miss Dotty, it was awful: there we would find them stuck up a chimney, alone and scared, knees and elbows torn and bloodied, and it would be our task to rescue them back down again. But too often we would arrive too late to find them beyond our saving, stuck tight in the chimneys, or burned by fire."

Dotty sat, aghast. "Oh but that's terrible, Pip!" she cried.

"And there was worse to come." Pip lamented. "Soon the rogue sweeps began to run out of young sweep folk to send up the chimneys.

Chapter 7

So they hatched a dreadful plan. Every sweep knows that ordinary folk can't travel through the chimneys without magick – even if they have a sweep with them. But armed with a chimney key it is a different matter. As long as you ordinary folk carry a chimney key about your person you can travel through the chimneys just like a sweep can. The rogue sweeps realised that they could use the chimney keys to force ordinary folks up their own chimneys, spiriting them into the world of the sweeps and to a world of terrible enslavement at the rogue sweeps' hands," continued Pip.

"So, one by one, the rogue sweeps began to enter the houses of the ordinary folk, stealing their precious chimney keys. Once in possession of a chimney key, the rogue sweeps could come down a person's chimney in the dead of night, taking the ordinary folks' children from their beds and forcing them up the chimneys, off into the world of sweeps to work as chimney boys and girls. The rumours that had started all this mess gave them the perfect cover, of course, as the ordinary folk expected nothing but trouble from us sweeps by then."

"Oh that's just awful, Pip," said Dotty.

"Anyway, I forget where I was," said Pip, returning to his story. "Ah yes. You may have noticed that us sweeps tend to be a bit smaller in stature than you ordinary folk," he continued. "So the rogue sweeps made it their practice to starve the ordinary children they took, to stop them from growing too big to get up the chimneys." Pip sighed heavily. "I tell you, Miss Dotty, it brings a tear to my eye what they did to those poor little ordinary boys and girls."

"The Sweeps' Council had to put a stop to it. They banned chimney hopping by anyone but an authorised sweep, and forbade all sweeps from making new chimney keys. Most of the existing keys were returned and destroyed by the Council, but a handful still remains. Of those known still to exist, all but one is in the safekeeping of the Sweeps' Council. But the key that belonged to this house, the Calendar House Key, is still missing." Dotty gasped. "And I have been tasked to find it," Pip concluded with a flourish.

"So who owned the key?" questioned Dotty. "Was it one of my ancestors?"

"It was your mother, Gwennie, who had it," replied Pip. "And I have to say I was rather hoping you might know something about it; but I can see now that you don't." Clearly Pip was disappointed. "When she moved away the Council thought it was lost: taken away with her to Wales. But then after your mother's untimely death, rumours started to fly amongst the sweeps that it might have been left here all the time, somewhere in the House. Now the rogue sweeps are looking for it."

Pip turned to Dotty "And so you see, Miss Dotty, that is why it is of such grave importance that I find the missing key. If that key should find its way into the wrong hands it could lead to the enslavement of countless innocent children by the rogue sweeps, and the small shred of trust that still remains between the world of sweeps and the ordinary folk will be lost forever."

"But is that likely, Pip?" Dotty asked. "Are there really those who would unearth the missing key and use it to *steal* innocent children?"

"Most have gone, Miss Dotty. Given up and gone in search of another wicked living, But there are two that remain' said the little sweep. 'They are the most evil of rogues; a truly terrible pair. They go by the names Porguss and Poachling. And they search for the key right now, in this very house."

Dotty shuddered at the thought of these strange and frightening characters wandering loose in the chimneys of the Calendar House. Even their names sounded creepy. It made her feel unsafe.

"So the noises in the chimneys: all the scratching and the scraping," Dotty had to ask; although she wasn't at all sure she wanted to hear the answer. "Was that you, Pip, or was it...*them*?"

Pip thought for a moment. "In truth, Miss Dotty, I would guess it's a bit of both you've been hearing, although as I said earlier, I've been away these past few days."

"Well as a matter of fact I haven't heard the noises so much since your last visit," said Dotty, forming a grim smile. "Gobby…I mean, the cook, Mrs Gobbins: she told me the noises were Jackdaws in the chimneys! I knew I was right not to believe her."

"Well she weren't exactly lying to you as it 'appens, Miss Dotty, although she may not have realised as such." Pip explained: "The rogue sweeps are in the habit of using jackdaws to do their spying for them. They are plentiful of course and can gain easy access through the chimneys without the use of magick which, together with their sooty appearance, makes them pretty much undetectable. Porguss and Poachling may well have been using them to scout out the house. You haven't come across any, I suppose?"

"No," replied Dotty. "I haven't seen anyone. I've just heard the noises. I half thought I was imagining things. Do you think they will be looking for me?" Dotty was really scared now.

"No, Miss, there's no reason for them to, not unless they have reason to believe you have knowledge of its whereabouts. Hey, I don't suppose there is any chance you could have it in your possession without realising it, could you, Miss Dotty? Your mother didn't give you anything for safekeeping, a trinket of some kind?" Pip looked hopeful for a moment.

"I'm afraid not, Pip," Dotty replied. "They died so suddenly. And pretty much everything we owned was destroyed in the blaze." Dotty felt wretched. She wished that her mother had been given those few precious moments to hand her a keepsake; that there was something she could do to help Pip.

"I really am so sorry, Miss." Pip removed his dirty black cap to show his respect. In doing so he revealed an almost perfect circle of dirty blond hair that had escaped the soot of the chimneys. It looked comical. Dotty laughed despite herself.

Pip looked at her quizzically. "Is something funny, Miss Dotty?"

"No, Pip. It's nothing, really." Dotty smiled.

"Right you are then, Miss." Pip continued. "I saw your place, you know. It got hit pretty bad by the fire, didn't it?"

"What?" Dotty spluttered. "You've been to Wyvern Road? You mean you've seen my home in Cardiff?" Not for the first time since meeting Pip Dotty's head was beginning to spin.

"Yes," said the boy. "The Council thought Gwennie, your mother, might have hidden the key there somewhere. I was tasked to check it out but I couldn't get in through the chimney: it was too damaged in the fire. So the Council sent me and a couple of the other apprentisweeps down there on foot."

Now Dotty was angry. What right did these people, these sweeps, have poking around in the ashes of her beloved Wyvern Road. "Well did you think of asking me?" demanded Dotty, enraged. "Didn't you think it might have been polite to ask before you went raiding my home?"

"But that's exactly what I was sent to do the other day, Miss Dotty. I would have asked you, truly, but you was so busy screaming I couldn't get a word in." Dotty couldn't really argue with that, so she stayed silent. She didn't feel any less cross about it though. It seemed very unfair that Pip had been given the chance to visit her home town and that she, Dotty, had not.

"Anyways," said Pip. "We couldn't find anything. Most likely the key's been destroyed, but we had to be sure."

"Well that's something, I suppose," Dotty snapped.

"I was only following orders, Miss Dotty. Please understand that," Pip pleaded. "In any case, I have my own theory."

"Which is?" Dotty required of him angrily.

"Well," ventured Pip. "I don't think your mother would have taken it with her when she left. There would have been no point. After all, if she had tried to use it the Council would have been straight onto her, asking for its return; and your mother wasn't one for sentimental keepsakes. No, I think that your mother must have hidden it here: somewhere in the house."

Pip's right, Dotty thought. Her mum was not one for sentimentality: she simply wouldn't have kept such a thing on a whim. Unless... Suddenly Dotty thought of the locket. *Could it be?* No of course not. Dotty dismissed the idea. The locket had no compartment inside; nothing that she could open. She had tried. No, this was something else. ...*But what about the picture of the boy on the back of the locket? Was he not a sweep?*

There was nothing for it. Dotty must tell Pip. If there was any chance at all that it was the missing Calendar House Key he needed to know right away. And furthermore Dotty needed to hide it again, and quick! She shuddered again at the thought of Porguss and Poachling getting their hands on the locket. It didn't bear thinking about.

"Pip, there's…" But as Dotty began to speak the drawing room's great door handle started to rattle. Pip turned sharply towards the noise.

"Dotty," Gobby shouted through the heavy wooden door. "Could you give me a hand, dear? I'm a little stuck."

Pip leaped to his feet. "Oh crikey, Miss, I'd better go!" he whispered.

"But, Pip, I…"

"Miss Dotty, don't you fret. There's plenty of other times I can answer your questions but for now I must leave."

"But there's something…" Dotty persisted. The door handle rattled more urgently.

"Dotty, are you there girl?" Gobby trilled.

"Now don't take on so, Miss. If you want me, ring the servants' bells next to the fireplaces. And I will be with you." Pip made to go.

"But they don't work. The bells don't work!" argued Dotty in whispers. "I've tried them. I've tried them all!" Dotty had made a point of ringing every bell in the house as she discovered its many rooms, but none of them made a sound.

"Just ring the bell and I will be with you," hushed Pip. "Never you fear." And with that, broom aloft, quick as a flash he ran to the chimney.

"But, Pip, I've got something to tell..." Dotty trailed off. It was too late. He was already gone.

The drawing room door burst open, with a great clamoring and clattering of china. It was Gobby with the tea things; a great big tray brimming with scones and jam and fresh butter and cream, and a jug of hot cocoa, its sweet smelling steam filling the room.

"Ah there you are, dear. Why ever did you not help me when I called? I nearly dropped the tray all over. Now there are scones and jam and..."

As Gobby bustled around with the tea things, chattering away, Dotty thought about what Pip had told her. Could she really help solve her mother's mystery? Could she help to find the key? She resolved to help in any way she could, although she had a sneaking suspicion she wasn't going to have to look very far to find it. If Dotty was right, the missing key was already in her possession.

Chapter 8

The Imaginary Friend

*In which Dotty tries to chimney hop and Strake delivers a
letter*

"Aren't you a bit old to have an imaginary
friend?" conjectured Sylv, eyebrow raised in
disapproval. Sylv was sulking because Dotty was
late to speak to her on Skype and Sylv didn't like
to be kept waiting: especially on account of what
she considered to be a figment of Dotty's
imagination.

"He's not imaginary, I tell you, he's real!"
Dotty was beginning to wish she hadn't
mentioned the sweep's existence to her friend at
all.

"Well whatever he is, just don't mention him to the social worker, okay?" Sylv cautioned.

"I'm telling you he'll have a field day," continued Sylv. Dotty pulled a face.

"Can't you just imagine it?" Sylv teased. "Social Worker Snoops, saying: *It would appear, Mr Winchester, that Dorothea has invented an imaginary friend.*" Sylv put on a funny voice. *"We are naturally concerned that this is a reaction to her isolated situation and clearly is something that we need to monitor closely over the coming months."*

"Stop it, Sylv, just stop it!" Dotty wailed.

"Alright, Dot, keep your hair on," Sylv answered. "I don't know. I think you've lost your sense of humour since you went to live 'Up North'. You used to be able to take a joke." Sylv continued, serious now. "All I'm saying, Dot, is that I know you're lonely but I don't think inventing an imaginary friend – this sweep character of all things - is going to do you any good, that's all." Dotty's friend eyed her with concern.

"But he's not imaginary, he's not he's not!" Dotty retorted, tears of indignation welling in her eyes.

"Seriously, Dot, listen to yourself." Sylv was getting impatient now. "You have a chimney sweep for a friend and you don't know where he comes from but he pops down the chimney to visit you. I mean, really?"

Dotty was crushed. "I can't believe you're calling me a liar! After all we've been through, you and me. I thought out of everyone you'd believe me." She trailed off.

"Alright," said Sylv. "Look, let's just leave it for now, shall we? Anyway, I've got better things to think about at the moment. My dad got totally spooked because there have been kids lurking around in your old house. Dad said they were rummaging around in the wreck, looking for something they could salvage and sell, most likely."

Dotty's ears pricked up. "Really?" she said.

"Yeah. Dad said they were filthy dirty," continued Sylv. "Must have been kicking about in the rubble for ages before he chased them off."

"The sweeps," Dotty murmured. "They were there, just like Pip said."

"What's that?" asked Sylv. "You mumbled. I didn't hear you."

"Oh nothing," Dotty's thoughts were elsewhere now.

"Anyway, it's left him a bit unsettled. He even asked Mum if I can go home and spend Christmas with him for once. Don't know if she will let me though. Dot, are you listening?"

Dotty wasn't. "Sorry, Sylv. Look, I've gotta go. Things to do…"

"Oh don't be like that, Dot. I was only teasing about your friend. You know I loves you," Sylv wheedled. But Dotty had signed off.

Dotty grabbed the locket from her bedside drawer and shoved it in her pocket. She wanted to take another look at it. But not in her bedroom with its big open fireplace; she wanted to be somewhere secret, somewhere safe. Mam's Playroom always seemed to have a sense of peace surrounding it: feeling somehow impenetrable from the strange goings on of the Calendar House. Dotty made her way there, suddenly feeling the need for caution.

There was a rocking chair in one corner of the playroom, painted white, with a big checked woollen rug draped over one arm. Dotty grabbed the rug and settled down on the floor with it, making herself comfortable next to the doll's house. She turned the locket over in her hands, examining it in detail. Once again the pendant filled her with amazement, not just because this was something that had been touched all those years ago by her mum's small hands, but now too because of the magic that it might somehow possess.

The locket was pretty. It was made of gold: not too large but heavy and solidly made. The front was set with tiny seed pearls and emeralds that caught the light as she moved it. On the back, encased in a circle of glass was the picture of the dirty little boy. Dotty had wondered if it might be Pip, but looking at it again it was clear that it wasn't him: the features of the boy in the picture were quite different to Pip's. Besides, it couldn't be him: if the locket had belonged to her mum, which Dotty was now sure it had, the boy in the picture would be grown up by now and Pip was still a boy. *Perhaps sweeps don't grow up in the same way as ordinary boys and girls do?* she cogitated. She would have to ask.

Dotty checked the locket again to see if it had any sort of compartment in it, but there was none that she could see. She shook it and put it to her ear. She didn't really know why; she supposed she wanted to see if it had any sort of reaction to her handling of it. Nothing happened.

"Oh fiddlesticks," Dotty muttered to herself. She was never going to find an answer just by staring at it. She simply needed to show the locket to Pip and have done with it. After all, surely the little sweep knew what he was looking for. He would be able to tell her straight away whether her mother's locket was the elusive key he and the rest of the sweep world had been hunting. Mind made up, Dotty strode over to the fireplace, glancing again at its pretty cast iron range, the fish dancing as the sunlight caught the iron scales upon their backs. Now, what had Pip said? Just to ring the bell, she remembered.

Dotty knew the bell didn't work, she had tried it before. Like most nine and a half year olds, if there was a bell to pull or a button to press she could not resist the urge to press it. The house had a bell of sorts next to every fireplace in the house, from what Dotty had seen. This was nothing unusual in grand old houses, of course, bells being necessary in the old days for the lords and ladies of the house to call their servants to assist them. And the bells in the Calendar House came in all different guises. Some were like a big old-fashioned doorbell: a brass plate with a circular button in the middle, worn smoother than smooth with years of pressing. Others had little rings or handles that you had to pull; and some were great ropes with huge tassels of brightly coloured silk weighing them down, that made Dotty feel like a church bell ringer when she pulled them.

Despite all her pressing, tugging and pulling, though, Dotty was yet to find a bell in the house that made a sound when she did so. Still, Pip was clear in his orders so, without hesitation Dotty pushed the button to the side of the playroom fireplace and waited for an answer. Nothing happened. Feeling impatient, she pressed again repeatedly. Still nothing.

"Oh, this is pointless," Dotty told off the silent bell, sticking her tongue out at it for good measure.

Thrusting the locket back into her jumper pocket, Dotty glumly left her mum's playroom behind and made her way back to her bedroom. Disappointment weighed heavily on her as she trudged along the corridor. Reaching her room, Dotty threw herself onto the bed. "Ouch!" she exclaimed. The locket dug into her as she landed, grazing her side through her jumper. Grumpily Dotty fished in her pocket for the offending item.

"You're the cause of all this!" she told the locket off, wagging a finger at it as if it were a naughty child. "If it weren't for you none of this would have happened! Oh what am I doing?" Dotty asked herself. With disappearing chimney sweeps and magic jewellery no wonder Sylv thought she was going crazy. "Perhaps I am," Dotty muttered. She eyed the locket crossly. She had arrived at the Calendar House with little enough, but at least she had her friend Sylv to keep her company, albeit virtually. Now they had fallen out and Dotty had nothing: nothing except an overweight spaniel and an imaginary (and very unreliable) friend for company. And as for the locket...

Dotty made as if to throw the locket away, to cast it into a far corner of her bedroom, to disgrace it; to hide it from view. But, remembering the locket belonged to her mum, she couldn't do it. Instead she held the locket close, clutching it to her heart and fell back into the bed, sighing as she did so. "Huh. Magic lockets," she grumbled to herself.

Then a thought struck her. Dotty didn't need Pip to tell her if this was the missing key at all. She could find out all by herself. Dotty could try it! Filled with new resolve, Dotty put the chain around her neck and hopped down off the high feather bed. "After all, what harm can it do?" she persuaded herself. She would stand in the fireplace and see if she got whizzed off anywhere. Most likely nothing would happen at all. Having proved that the locket was nothing more a nice piece of jewellery, she could go back to enjoying the thing as something to remember her mother by, and not some strange thing of magic to be awed and feared, even. Without further ado, Dotty stepped into the fireplace.

The weight of the locket was heavy around her neck. Dotty waited. A strange wind stirred in the chimney. There was a crackle of electricity in the air, making the hairs on the back of Dotty's neck bristle. Dotty felt the air around her become almost tangible: whispering to her; taking breath. The prickle of electricity bounced around in the chimney opening, first up and then down, tickling the underside of her feet, lifting her heels from the floor. There was a sharp knock at the bedroom door. Dotty stepped out of the fireplace.

She couldn't believe it. How was it that with so few people living in the house someone always managed to interrupt her when something important was about to happen? Couldn't she be given a moment's peace? To heap injury upon insult, whoever had been knocking at the door didn't wait for Dotty to answer, either, and the door at once began to open. She was less than pleased to see that the knocking had come from Strake. Her great uncle's sinister secretary stalked into the room, balancing at the end of his long spidery fingertips a silver tray on which was placed a single letter, addressed to Dotty.

Remembering the locket around her neck, Dotty grabbed it and shoved it under her jumper to conceal it. But it seemed she was not quick enough: Strake had already seen it. He tried to hide it but a flicker of recognition swam across his features. In the split second it took for him to regain his composure the silver tray he was holding wobbled, almost imperceptibly. Strake cleared his throat, rasping with a painful croak that sounded like sandpaper against glass.

"Ahem. Miss Parsons, a letter for you. From your great uncle, if I'm not mistaken."

Strake's eyes bored into Dotty hungrily, and for a moment she was sure he meant to devour her.

"Er, thank you," stammered Dotty. She looked at the letter, afraid that if she reached out to take it Strake might grab her: grab the locket. Steeling herself, Dotty took a step forward, reaching out quickly and snatching the letter from the silver tray. Strake did not move a muscle but stood perfectly still, like a venomous snake waiting to strike.

Dotty really wanted him to leave the room now. "Is that all?" she asked, pointedly.

Strake continued to stand, rooted to the spot like a stubborn weed. His eyes searched across the length of chain visible around Dotty's neck. It was as if he was trying to look through her, seeking confirmation of what she was hiding.

Dotty repeated herself, a little more loudly this time. "The letter, Mr Strake. Is that all?" Strake flinched, as if awaking from a daydream. "Ah, yes, Miss Parsons, that is all." The queer man looked at Dotty with what she thought was a knowing look and retreated from the room, backwards as always, closing the door behind him.

Dotty gulped for air. What had just happened? Did Strake really know about the Calendar House Key or was she just being paranoid? If he did, Dotty was certain Strake meant to do no good with it. And, more importantly, before his poorly timed entrance had she really been about to fly up the chimney?

But there was something else that required her attention now. Realising that she still clutched the unopened letter in her hand, Dotty quickly tore a corner from the envelope. Wiggling her finger into the hole and using it like a letter opener, she tore all the way along the letter's longest side, freeing its contents. Strake had been right. It was a letter from her great uncle.

"Dearest Girl" it read.

"I am so sorry to have missed you this last week, but I have good news for you now. My business in London is nearly concluded and I

hope to return to you on the afternoon of the 24th, just in time for the Christmas festivities. I am so looking forward to renewing our acquaintance.

With fondest wishes
Your Great Uncle, Winchester x

p.s. I do hope Geoff is keeping you company and not getting into too much trouble with Mrs Gobbins".

Christmas Eve; but that was only three days away! Dotty felt a flood of relief. She was sure that her great uncle would be able to untangle all this mess for her, even if it was only by telling her that she had indeed gone completely bonkers.

In the meantime, there was much she had to do. Dotty had to hide the locket, and fast.

The Imaginary Friend

Chapter 9

Porguss and Poachling

In which Dotty has a nasty encounter with two rogue sweeps

Something wasn't right. It was as if some strange magic had been unleashed when Dotty had stepped into the chimney with the locket. The crackle of electricity that she felt in the fireplace had gone, but it had left behind it a charge, some sort of unseen force: an electrical current that lingered in the air. Dotty felt it all around her and it made the hairs on her forearms stand to attention, like goose bumps from the cold.

Worse than this, though, the scratching had stopped. Dotty should have been pleased with this turn of events, but she wasn't. The Calendar

House was eerily quiet and that made her very nervous indeed. Dotty was quite sure that the noises in the chimneys had ceased at the same time the electricity started. The question was, why? No matter how hard she tried Dotty couldn't shake the growing suspicion that it was because *they* had found her out. In stepping into the fireplace with that locket around her neck Dotty had somehow unlocked the power that had for so many years lain hidden inside it. Yes, that must be it. *They* knew there was no longer any need to look for the Calendar House Key because *they* knew that Dotty had it.

Dotty had hidden the locket in the safest place she could think of; not in the fireplace where she had found it, but somewhere else; somewhere that she hoped nobody would think to look. Nevertheless, she was in constant fear of its discovery. Every creak of a floorboard, every unexpected shadow, made her leap half out of her skin. Dotty couldn't shake the feeling that whatever she had awakened was now watching her. Watching and waiting.

And as if the quiet presence in the house wasn't enough, Strake was acting very strangely too. Suddenly ever-present in her daily routines, Dotty saw Strake wherever she went. The man seemed to be lurking around every corner, waiting in the shadows, staring at her with his beady little eyes, surveying her every move; his very form questioning her.

Chapter 9

Dotty couldn't bear it: even Mam's Playroom didn't feel like quite the safe haven it once had been. She resorted to avoiding the house as she had done when she first heard the scratchings in the chimney, and the garden once again became her welcome refuge.

Kicking about in the garden with Geoff wasn't all bad. The daft antics of the overweight spaniel formed a welcome distraction from the strange goings-on in the house and, well, the fact of the matter was that Dotty rather enjoyed his unquestioning company. The weather had worsened rapidly over the last few days and rain and wind turned to ice and snow, making a winter wonderland of the gardens. Everything gleamed white and fresh and the cold crispness of the air was clean and pure. There was nothing complicated here; nothing hidden. The garden felt safe.

There was a down-side of course: Dotty had to stop using her roller blades, outside at least. The fresh powdered snow clogged up her wheels and, despite Kenny clearing the footways with grim efficiency, there was just too much ice on the paths to risk it. Nonetheless, Dotty still enjoyed tromping around outside in her boots, wrapped up against the winter cold, watching Geoff lolloping about and rolling in the snow. Again and again the spaniel would cover himself from head to toe in the fresh white powder, transforming himself into a four-legged snowman before shaking it all off, covering Dotty in icy, wet slush.

Dotty was up early. It was a fine crisp day and a fresh snow shower during the night had left the garden unspoilt by footprints. The frost sparkled like diamond dust on every twig and branch in the early morning light. Dotty threw on her clothes and raced down the back stairs. No-one was up yet, not even Gobby. As she darted through the empty kitchen it seemed strange not seeing the cook in her usual place at the kitchen table. Reaching the boot room, Dotty collected coat, hat, scarf and a very sleepy Geoff. He had taken up residence in the boot room ever since his master's absence; it seemed it was the nearest the greedy spaniel could get to the kitchen without a telling-off from Gobby.

"Come on, Geoff, you lazy mutt!" Dotty pulled at Geoff's collar impatiently. "Come on, let's go! There's a whole world to explore out there before breakfast." Geoff yawned, stretching slowly as if to make a point, and then lumbered over to the door. "Geoff, you really are the most idle dog," she grumbled.

Once in the garden Geoff perked up, sniffing about for the scent of a rabbit and wagging his stub of a tail as he did so. Dotty looked down towards the lake. There was little wind and the water was very still today. The lake looked as if it was beginning to freeze over. The pair made their way towards the water, taking a fairly direct route, stopping and starting as Geoff investigated along the way. Reaching the water's edge, Dotty saw that she was right: the lake had all but frozen over, the ducks fighting for space in which to preen and bob between the patches of ice. The lake was beautiful, she thought.

For a moment a moving cloud blocked out the sun and Dotty suddenly felt very cold. Shivering, she turned back towards the house. There was a solitary bird circling above the rooftops. It was a jackdaw. Dotty watched with unease as the jackdaw alighted silently in all its grey-black splendour on top of one of the many chimney pots. The bird started tapping at the pot: *tap! Tap tap tap! Tap taaap*! It sounded as if it was tapping out a message. No, it couldn't be. *Don't be daft girl*. Dotty reassured herself. *You're seeing signs where there are none*. Shaking the thought from her head Dotty turned back towards the lake, but the sight of the bird had unsettled her and the view no longer held its magic.

"Oh, Pip, where are you?" she cried across the water. Why had he not come when she had rung the fireside bell in Mam's Playroom? He had promised it would work! How could he be so mean, staying hidden when she so desperately needed to find him? Then Dotty had a thought. Perhaps she should try to ring the servants' bell again. Maybe it was just like ringing a doorbell and Pip had simply been out when she had called before. There was no time to waste, she would go back into the house and try it right away.

"Here, Geoff! Come on boy. Let's go back inside and see if we can steal a treat for you from Gobby." Geoff panted in agreement, wagging his tail enthusiastically at the thought of food. Together the pair began the long walk up the hill towards the Calendar House. As they trudged along Dotty glanced up again at the roof to see if the jackdaw was still there. At first she couldn't see it. She heaved a sigh of relief, but then she saw not one, but two jackdaws, perching together on a different chimney pot. Dotty fancied they were watching her. Suddenly she wanted nothing more than to get indoors: into the warmth and safety of Gobby's kitchen.

The ascent back up to the house was a quick one, Geoff being spurred on at the promise of a stolen treat from the kitchen. As they reached the back door the welcome scent of Gobby's morning toil reached out through the chill air to greet them.

"I think you're in luck, Geoff," said Dotty. "Smells like she's cooking meat." Geoff salivated, a string of doggy drool starting to form at one corner of his mouth. "Now stay behind me, boy, until I give you the all-clear. Okay?" Geoff wagged his tail in assent, the length of dribble elongating. Dotty trotted into the kitchen. She had been right: Gobby was baking a steak pie for dinner. What a result!

Chapter 9

By now well-practiced in the art of kitchen thievery, the duo launched a two-pronged assault on the unsuspecting cook, Geoff sneaking up to the kitchen work bench and snaffling the fat trimmings off the meat whilst Dotty kept Gobby occupied in pleasant morning conversation. Gobby chattered away merrily. She was always happy when she was baking.

"I'm going to make spiced gingerbread when I've got this pie in the oven, Dotty," she trilled. "I always make a gingerbread house for the Christmas table. Would you like to help me? It's one of my favourite things to make." Dotty smiled. If Dotty had to count up all of Gobby's favourite things to make she would have to use every finger and every toe to do so, and probably still be in need of more. Gobby just loved cooking.

"Oh I'm sorry Mrs Gobbins but I have things to do this morning. I need to go visit Mam's Playroom."

Gobby looked crushed. "I understand, dear," she said, clearly not understanding. "Well maybe you might like to help me decorate it this afternoon, once the gingerbread has cooled? That's the best bit anyway." The cook brightened at the thought. "I've got icing and jelly tots and liquorice string and glazed cherries and sweet angelica and…"

"That would be great," Dotty interjected. "Thanks, Mrs Gobbins." Without further ado,

Dotty negotiated her way out of the kitchen, ushering Geoff past the unsuspecting Gobby. For such a bumbling oaf of a dog, Geoff could be remarkably stealthy when the need arose.

As soon as she was out of sight, Dotty raced towards Mam's Playroom, running helter-skelter up the back stairs with Geoff panting along behind her. Upon reaching her destination, she closed the playroom door cautiously behind her, Geoff sealing the door shut with his furry oversized doggy behind. She could trust no-one now; no-one except Pip, and Geoff of course. Dotty picked through the playroom furniture, past the doll's house, towards the range that filled the fireplace.

As she crossed the room past the window a shadow on the glass caught her eye, making her start. It was a jackdaw perching on the window ledge. The bird stared at her with one bright beady little eye, cocking its head as if in greeting. Dotty shrieked and, grabbing the curtain in both hands, pulled it across the window, shutting out both the bird and the sunlight as one. She shuddered. The usually bright sunny room was surprisingly dark with the curtain closed and the room was at once filled with shadow, making it eerie in the half-light. Dotty could have snapped on the light but there wasn't a moment to lose.

Taking the last two steps towards the fireplace Dotty reached forward and pressed the servant's bell. There was no sound, but this was to be expected. None of the bells worked. Frantically, she pressed the bell again, and then again and again. "Pip, where are you?" she called. But it was no use. Dotty knew instinctively that Pip simply wasn't coming. Angry now, Dotty turned on her heel, striding across the room to open the door. She didn't wait for Geoff to move, she just shunted him out of the way with the door as she opened it. "Come on, Geoff, let's go," she uttered darkly. "There's nothing for us here."

Back in her bedroom, Dotty slumped down on her bed, Geoff taking up his usual position by the door. "Oh, Geoff," complained Dotty bitterly. "Maybe Sylv is right. Perhaps I should forget all about Pip and the Calendar House Key and find something else to occupy my time. After all, school is starting soon, and there's Christmas coming and…"

Dotty cut herself short, surprised. A strange noise was emanating from Geoff: a noise Dotty had never heard him make before. Geoff was growling. As Dotty watched the usually harmless animal with increasing alarm, she saw that Geoff was no longer watching her. The docile and patient expression he usually wore was gone completely and in its place was one of fierce warning. Geoff stood rigid at the doorway, every muscle taught, his fur bristling, teeth bared, his mouth twisted into a snarl. Geoff's eyes were focused, not upon Dotty, but to a space behind her, fixed upon the fireplace. A low snarl rumbled in his throat. Dotty turned.

The rumbling increased, but it did not now come from Geoff. The chimney breast was emitting an awkward crunching grinding sound, slow and heavy, like huge blocks of stone creaking and moving with great force. Dotty watched, breathless and unmoving. The chimney breast bulged as if it were straining with the effort of expelling its cargo onto the hearth. Something big was coming; and that something had feet – four feet to be precise! Dotty stood transfixed as the fireplace spewed out its contents.

Slowly Dotty's eyes began to make sense of the huge globular form as it settled on her bedroom hearth. Dotty now realised that what she was witnessing was the appearance of not one person, but two. It was like watching a pair of giant slugs oozing from the fireplace. So large and amorphous was their shape that it was at first difficult to tell one from the other, or to separate their features. But she knew at once that this pair needed no introduction. There was no doubt in her mind that the bulging mass now occupying her fireside rug was the twin forms of the dreaded rogue sweeps themselves: Porguss and Poachling.

Presently, one of the pair spoke. "Greetings, Sister," she simpered, her smile showing two rows of sharp, jagged little teeth, their pointed edges surprising within such a round exterior. "We see that you know us already," she oozed, "so perhaps a formal introduction is unnecessary. But in any case I am Mistress Porguss and my companion here is Master Poachling."

Poachling surveyed Dotty with piggy little eyes, his fat sausage fingers resting on his great waistcoated belly. His look was one of displeasure. He clearly considered the meeting an inconvenience. Porguss continued, elbowing Poachling as she did so, as if to nudge him into a smile as similarly insincere as her own. Remembering himself, Poachling smiled at Dotty. Dotty wished he hadn't.

"Sister," the woman continued breathily. "It has come to our attention that you may be in receipt of something we want. Something we have need of. A trinket, if you like."

Porguss spread out towards her. "Tell me good Sister, have you seen such a thing?" The smile widened. Dotty thought Porguss looked as if she might eat her.

Dotty had never been more scared. "No," she replied in a small voice. "I don't have anything like that."

She held her breath. Dotty knew exactly what they wanted. Could they know that she was lying?

"Come now, Sister, now don't be like that." Porguss' smile faded, her look more sinister now.

"Just hand me the key and we will be on our way."

Dotty jutted her chin out defiantly, trying to be brave. "No, really, I don't know what you are talking about."

"Mistress Porguss," Poachling interjected. "Enough of your trifling with the child. Your niceties simply stand in our way."

Poachling turned to continue Dotty's interrogation. "Now look here, young Mistress," he snarled. "We need the Calendar Key and we need it now. Either you produce it for us forthwith or no end of harm will come to you," he menaced. And with remarkable speed the man's fat little fingers shot out and grabbed Dotty's arm, encircling her in their grasp, making her scream. Poachling drew Dotty to him, his greasy complexion dangerously close to hers. "Do you understand me?"

All at once there was a great kerfuffle as Geoff launched himself towards the offending pair with a flurry of barking, seeking them out with his teeth as he did so. "Argh!" screamed Porguss. "A dog! A dog! Quick, we must away. He will alert the household with his barking," she cried as she tried to shake him from her skirts. "Damn you, creature!"

Poachling offered Dotty a final menacing stare. "We will return, young Mistress, and when we do you had better have the locket ready for us."

Chapter 9

"Do what is best for you and give us the key, Sister," added Porguss. "Give us the key or you will live to regret it."

With that the pair slithered back up the chimney, plaster popping as they went, the brickwork of the chimney breast crunching and straining with their great girth; and all the while Geoff barked away behind them.

Porguss and Poachling

Chapter 10

Pip at Last!

In which Dotty finally speaks to Pip and is forced to make a confession

"Oh, Geoff, you're my hero!" Dotty grabbed the portly spaniel around the scruff of the neck and hugged him tightly. "I never thought you had it in you! You frightened those two off, good and proper."

Geoff wagged his tail, giving Dotty an appreciative lick across the face. "Yuck, Geoff! I don't love you that much!" she scolded, still smiling, and gave him another hug. Geoff nuzzled her with his big wet chocolate brown nose.

"Come on, boy, this calls for a celebration. Let's go downstairs and see if we can muster you a treat. If we go and see Gobby I'm sure I can sneak you some gingerbread." At this Geoff

wagged his tail with such enthusiasm that almost his entire back end wagged along with it.

In truth, Dotty's reasons for wanting to be back downstairs in the kitchen with Gobby were as much about the need for her to feel safe as they were for the purpose of procuring forbidden foodstuffs for Geoff. The meeting with Porguss and Poachling had left her shaken, and she was more than a little scared that they would return.

Still, she took comfort in the fact that Geoff's presence was such an obvious deterrent to the pair, and resolved that Geoff's sleeping arrangements would from now on be elevated from boot room to bedroom: Dotty's bedroom, to be precise.

Gobby beamed as Dotty alighted from the bottom step of the back staircase and into the kitchen and Dotty felt a gush of gratitude that she had the cook as an ally, albeit an unknowing one. Unfortunately the smile was short-lived, as it was quickly replaced with a scowl at the sight of Geoff.

"Dotty, dear, you know I don't like animals in my kitchen," she chided. "Hurry along now and be rid of him and then we can start with the icing. The gingerbread's just about cooled."

Geoff looked forlorn. Dotty reassured him. "You just go and have a sleep in the boot room and I'll come and get you when I'm finished." She led him reluctantly through the kitchen by his collar. "And don't fret," she whispered "I'll bring you something to make it worth your while."

Suitably reassured, Geoff trotted off through the kitchen door to seek out his favourite place under the shoe bench.

Dotty should have known that the gingerbread house Gobby was making would be far from an ordinary gingerbread house. It was more like a gingerbread mansion, or a gingerbread castle, than a plain old house. Dotty was happy just to watch in awe to begin with as Gobby worked on the grand undertaking, using the icing like glue, sticking and adding, walls and roofs and parapets and railings. It was quite the masterpiece.

Gobby worked quickly and skillfully, all the while chatting away gaily, as was her custom. Dotty found the cook's pleasant chirruping comforting after the drama of the morning's adventures, and she relaxed into the moment, watching Gobby piecing together the magnificent edible structure.

"Mr. Strake said that a letter had come for you, dear. From your Great Uncle Winchester, I believe?" Gobby did not look up as she talked; her focus was on a conical section of roof tower that was proving tricky to affix.

"Yes, Mrs Gobbins." Dotty had almost forgotten about the letter from her guardian.

"Did he say when he was planning on returning?" Gobby went on. "It's all very inconvenient his disappearing off like this, you know. I just can't plan the festivities properly until I know when he is due to arrive." The cook glowered at the sticky gingerbread tower; it clearly wasn't doing as it was told. "Mind you, she mused, he always has been one for taking off suddenly. Makes my life a misery! Never knowing what to cook…"

Dotty cut in: "The day after tomorrow he said, Mrs Gobbins."

"The day after tomorrow!" Gobby flung her hands into the air in alarm. "But that's Christmas eve!" The tower roof slid silently off its fixings, sagging down the wall as if it had too much to drink. "Well, I do say," Gobby set to putting the tower right, quietly efficient. "Talk about leaving it to the last minute. Still, I suppose we will just have to make do with that, won't we?" she harrumphed.

Dotty had to confess she was equally impatient for her great uncle's return. She had so many questions to ask him; so much still to be answered. And in the absence of Pip it seemed that Great Uncle Winchester was the only person who could fill in the gaps.

There was no time to think about it now though as at last Dotty's assistance was required in the kitchen. Woman and girl set about the task of decorating the gingerbread house as Gobby produced armfuls of adornments for it, from chocolate drops to dolly mixtures and from glazed fruit to little flags made of sugar paper and all manner of sugared treats to fill the stomach and feast the eyes in equal splendour.

Together Gobby and her gleeful assistant covered the rooftops with patterns, decorated the walls with sugar flowers and made a beautiful marzipan path right up to its gingerbread door. It truly was a sight to behold.

Finished, the pair stood back a while to inspect their efforts. "Good." Gobby nodded with satisfaction. "Thank you for your assistance, Dotty. Feel free to help yourself to some of the leftovers if you're peckish. They'll only go to waste." Dotty's eyes gleamed. Quick as a flash she filled her pockets with several gingerbread roundels and a handful of leftover sugar sweets. Geoff was going to love this.

Gobby smiled generously. "And now you'd best be on your way before I rope you into helping with the washing up."

Dotty needed no further encouragement than this to make her exit swift and, after collecting an impatiently waiting Geoff, they trudged off together through the house to find somewhere to share their spoils.

For obvious reasons Dotty didn't really fancy going back to her bedroom yet. In seeking an alternative the library seemed as good a choice as any. Dotty reasoned that, in the absence of suitable weather for garden tromping, immersing herself in a good book would be the most sensible course of action to take her mind off her latest predicament. Any fear of reprisals for gingerbread crumbs left on the rug from she and Geoff's impromptu afternoon feast were quickly assuaged by Geoff's enthusiastic cleaning up, as he licked every fibre of the carpet for stray morsels.

The pair were soon happily occupied, Dotty with her nose in a copy of an adventure novel and Geoff seeking out imaginary crumbs of food, all the real ones having long since been devoured. The time passed pleasantly and the afternoon began to turn to early evening, the shadows getting longer on the book shelves as the winter sun began to set over the hills beyond the house.

Dotty was in the middle of a particularly gripping chapter of her chosen book (*how could the heartless Marguerite give her husband away to that evil brute Chauvelin? Surely she must realise by now that Sir Percy was the hero of the piece!*), when a banging and a scratching began in the fireplace. Instantly Dotty looked to Geoff. He seemed not to have noticed the phenomenon. Perhaps it was just the wind whipping round the chimneys again.

But no, there was no mistaking it: a definite clamour in the chimney. Dotty jumped up, darting behind the sofa for all the protection it could give her. From her lookout she watched, fearful that it might be Porguss and Poachling returning for the Key.

But almost at once she knew that it was not. The noise in the chimney was different than it had been earlier that day. There was no creaking and groaning of the masonry as it stretched to give passage to the gargantuan pair. This was more of a tumble and a fall, the swish and a thump of a familiar small boy. It was Pip!

Announcing himself in his usual fit of flapping and coughing, Pip landed on the fireplace rug. The unmistakable smell of soot pervaded the room. "Afternoon, Miss!" he chirped, with his hallmark cheeky grin.

"Pip! Oh, Pip, it's you!" Dotty ran towards the boy, arms outstretched, hugging him as hard as can be. "Oh thank goodness, I've been so scared!"

Pip was a little taken aback by Dotty's outburst of affection. "Well I have to say, Miss, that's a vast improvement from your last two greetings, but it's hardly proper. You'll be getting me into trouble with Mr Winchester. And you're covered in soot!"

Dotty blushed. "Oh he's not here at the moment. He'll be back on Christmas Eve, he says. But never mind that for the moment. I have so much to tell you. Where on earth have you been? Why didn't you come when I rang the bell? I tried it twice!"

"Well as I keep trying to tell you, Miss Dotty, I've had important matters to attend to, and if you will keep ringing the wrong bell…"

"The wrong bell? But you told me to ring any bell!" Dotty retorted.

"Well, yes, any bell with an open fireplace," said the sweep. "But you can't be expecting me to come down a chimney with a cast iron cooking range in it, surely? Can you imagine what sort of mess that would make? The magick wouldn't know which way to send me and there would be nowhere for my poor legs and arms to go. What a terrible mess that would make! I'd be black and blue all over, and most likely quite stuck."

"Well yes I can see how that would be logical but…"

"But what?" Pip asked. "Oh *I see*! you're going to ask me the Santa Claus question aren't you?"

"The…what question?" Dotty was getting confused: not an uncommon occurrence when in Pip's company.

"Don't deny it," said the boy smugly. "Every one of you ordinary folk asks it. Just because he's our most famous sweep."

"Santa Claus is a sweep?" Dotty was dumbfounded.

"Yes, of course. That's obvious ain't it?" Pip shrugged. "How else do you think he travels up and down the chimneys? And the answer is he uses faerie magick."

"The answer to what? What do you mean he uses faerie magick? If he's a sweep why doesn't he use sweep's magick like all the other sweeps?" Now Dotty was really struggling to keep up.

"Well of course he *does* use sweep's magick to travel the chimneys," Pip rolled his eyes. "But like I just told you simple sweep's magick can't be used to come down a chimney without an open fire. For that you need faerie magick."

"Well that's as clear as mud," quipped Dotty.

"Really, Miss Dotty, it ain't complicated. If there's no open fireplace in the room Master Christmas uses a simple faerie charm to transport the room back to the time when there was an open fireplace in the house and then uses that for his passage." The boy sighed impatiently.

"That's all very fascinating I'm sure, Pip, and thank you for explaining it to me but I really can't see how it's relevant to our current situation and I have something very urgent to tell you. I think I might be in real danger!"

"Well why didn't you say so?" retorted the boy. And with that he threw himself onto the nearby sofa, hands laced behind his head, and crossed his dirty bare feet atop the coffee table. "Go on then, Miss Dotty, I'm all ears."

Dotty resisted the urge to quarrel with the feisty little sweep and sat down carefully in an adjacent chair, looking at him plainly. "It's just that I've found something, Pip; something hidden. And I think it's the Calendar House Key."

Now it was Pip's turn to look incredulous as Dotty slowly recounted the story of her discovery of the locket in the chimney, how she believed it had belonged to her mother; and of the dirty little boy on the rear of the casing that she felt must surely be a sweep.

"So do you think that could be it: the key that you are looking for?" asked Dotty of the boy. "Perhaps I should fetch it for you to have a look at."

"No need, Miss Dotty. That is most certainly it. I remember seeing it about your mother's neck many a time," said the boy solemnly. "But why didn't you tell me about this before? It would have saved me a lot of looking, you know. Me and many others, besides!"

"I'm sorry," said Dotty. "I tried to tell you but Gobby was at the door and you left before I could finish telling you. I've been trying to find you, to tell you, ever since." Dotty looked downcast. "And it's not been easy, you know. I've been all alone and my best friend thinks I've gone mad with all this talk of chimney sweeps and I've had no-one to share it with. Not even Great Uncle Winchester. Not even you." Dotty fiddled with her hands, trying not to cry.

Pip looked in sympathy at the crestfallen Dotty. "Now then, Miss, don't you fret." Pip soothed. "Your faithful servant and resident chimney sweep Master Pip is now here at your service and I *promise*, cross my heart," the boy made the sign of a cross with his forefinger over

his left breast as he spoke "that I won't leave you again without solace."

Dotty looked at Pip, wanting to believe him. Pip smiled at her reassuringly. "Now, Miss Dotty, it seems to me that what you need to brighten your mood is a change of scenery and I have just the very thing." The diminutive sweep jumped to his feet, a hint of Pip grin across his face. "Have you ever been ice skating?"

"Wow! No, I haven't," she replied eagerly.

"Then Ice skating we shall go," announced the boy. "Now, you said you had the Key hidden in a safe place?"

"Yes," said Dotty. "Well at least I think so. It's in as safe a place as I could think of."

"Okay," said Pip. "Then as long as it isn't used I think we should be okay for now. Come on then, let's be off and have some fun."

Dotty hesitated, looking away. Pip eyed her, his gaze questioning. "Miss Dotty, you have told me everything, haven't you? There's nothing more you want to get off your chest?" Suddenly Pip looked panicked. "Say, you haven't used it, have you, Miss Dotty? You haven't used the key?"

Dotty remained silent, avoiding his gaze. Fear spread across Pip's face like a rash.

"Please, Miss. Tell me you haven't. Tell me you haven't stepped into the fireplace with that locket!"

"I didn't go anywhere," Dotty resisted. "I just stood there for a moment." Dotty felt like a rabbit in the headlights. She was going to have to tell him about *them*.

"Okay," said Pip, thinking aloud. "Well you obviously didn't use the key or the magick would have been unlocked and Porguss and Poachling would have found you for sure. Just keep the key hidden for now and whatever you do, do not be tempted to use it. If you do they are sure to come looking for you and then you really will be in danger."

"Oh Pip, I'm so sorry. I'm afraid it's too late," gushed Dotty. "They already have come looking. And I've already seen them. Here in the Calendar House."

Dotty recalled her frightening experience, recounting to Pip the events of the last days, of Strake seeing the necklace and of her certainty of his suspicions; of the hideous and threatening twin forms of Porguss and Poachling and of the jackdaws congregating on the roof outside.

"This is the worst possible news," said Pip grimly. "Ice skating will have to wait. I must alert the Sweeps' Council immediately. We cannot use the chimneys now. We have to find another way to get the key out of the house; to return it to the Council without being caught."

Chapter 10

Now it was Dotty's turn to console and hearten Pip. "Don't worry, Pip," Dotty reassured him. "I think I have a plan. I just need a little bit of time to check something: to set it up."

"Thank you, Miss, but time is something we just don't have. Best leave it to the Council," Pip sighed.

"But I'm sure I can help, Pip. Truly." Dotty urged. "Just give me until tomorrow evening. I'm pretty sure I can do it by then."

"Okay, Miss, if you really can help. But at the first sign of trouble we have to let them know, to call them for aid. It's just too serious a matter to leave to chance or fate." Pip walked to the fireplace, his countenance sober now. "Okay, Miss Dotty. The Sweeps are counting on you. Good luck." he said, and in an instant he was back up the chimney, out of sight and to who knows where to alert the Sweep's Council.

And with that the fate of the magical world of the sweeps, and the safety of little boys and girls everywhere was left in the hands of an orphaned nine and a half year old girl from Cardiff.

Pip at Last!

Chapter 11

What is Strake Up To?

In which Strake gives Dotty the slip and Sylv agrees to help with her plan

It was now dark but this wasn't a task that could wait until morning.

Dotty knew that dinner would be any time soon, so she decided to hold on until after she had eaten to do it. There would be less chance of her being disturbed that way in any case. Not waiting to be called to supper, Dotty made her own way to the kitchen and professed hunger to Gobby, hoping to bring forward the timing of her meal, even if only by a little. As it was she was actually too preoccupied with her plan for returning the Calendar House Key to the Sweeps' Council to eat anything much. Even Gobby's mince and onion with carrots and dumplings, a firm favourite of Dotty's in the cold winter weather, fell short of the mark. Much to Gobby's surprise and disappointment, Dotty declined a second helping of the savoury mince and altogether refused the jam roly poly and custard offered to her by way of dessert.

Gobby clucked at her "I hope you're not pining over anything, dear. It's unlike you not to eat," she fussed. "I tell you what, I'll plate up a portion of roly poly and custard for you. You can always have it before bed. You're bound to be peckish by then." Having satisfied herself that her charge would be thus well-catered for, Gobby left Dotty to her own devices and Dotty was free to put her sleuthing into action, as she had promised Pip.

As soon as the meal was over, Dotty ran to the boot room and collected Geoff, donning her roller blades as she did so. "Come on, Geoff," she said "You can be my wing man." She felt like a spy on a mission. "Let's go and stake out Strake."

Her roller blades might be speedy but they did not, Dotty quickly realised, give her the edge in terms of stealth. As she skated along the corridor the plastic wheels bumped and glided over the parquet flooring, clattering and echoing around the walls of the large empty corridors. It didn't matter though, Dotty told herself. As long as Strake didn't realise what she was up to it really didn't matter whether or not he knew she was there. In fact what better excuse was there for lurking in the vacuous hallways of the Calendar House at night than a spot of pre-bedtime roller-blading?

Dotty had twice tried to gain access to Great Uncle Winchester's study in his absence, and on both occasions had been warded off by Strake. Moreover, Strake had been quite clear that he had no intention of letting the girl into the study unsupervised, or even at all, if he were to have his way. *Third time lucky,* Dotty told herself. She had to try, no matter what. She was sure that the key to everything lay in that study. If she could just get into the room and confirm her suspicions about the window that faced out onto the courtyard, the problem of getting the locket to the Council would be solved with no need to chimney hop and no risk of alerting Porguss and Poachling. She could just hand the locket to Pip through the window.

It was six-thirty. A clock in the hallway somewhere bonged, confirming the time and masking the sound of Dotty's wheels as she neared the study. The hallway was dimly lit with the help of an oriental lamp which sat on a low table in a wide alcove opposite the study door. The light glowed on the warm wooden paneling. The study door was ajar. Was there a faint light coming from the study too? Or was it just the glow from the lampshade? It was hard to tell. Dotty hoped the room was not occupied.

Gesturing to Geoff to sit, Dotty sidled up to the doorway, peering through the gap in the door for a better look inside. She crossed her fingers for luck. If only they were alone.

It was not good news, however: Strake was inside. The crooked man sat at her great uncle's desk, poring over some sort of ledger, the blind closed behind him covering the study window. She had hoped he would have finished his day's work by now, but much as she was disappointed to see him it seemed fitting that Strake should be there. He appeared to Dotty to be a creature of twilight, happiest when the shadows were long and the light was scarce, his very essence being nourished by all that was foreboding and strange. Balancing on the stoppers of her boots, as if on tiptoe, she watched him unknowing as he worked: poring over his books, long spidery fingers smudged black with ink, his face made more unnatural by the dim lamplight in which he laboured. Her very proximity to him sent shivers up her spine.

"Oh well," Dotty whispered to Geoff. "It just looks like we're going to have to wait." Clearly Strake wasn't planning on leaving any time soon, but he would have to leave eventually, she reasoned. The only question was when? Dotty settled down on the hall carpet, Geoff beside her, and waited, Strake all the while oblivious to her presence.

But Strake didn't leave the study. Dotty had to admit that she was getting pretty bored, and hungry besides. If only she had stopped for seconds of dinner. Still, at least she had the jam roly poly to look forward to at the end of her spying mission. Dotty watched and waited, the ticking clock in the hallway marking the slow passage of time with tortuous accuracy. As the clock bonged eight, caution gave way to boredom and Dotty took to skating up and down the hall as a means of passing the time. Her rather less than quiet pastime seemed not to bother Strake though, not once looking up from his books to question her presence outside in the corridor.

As the time elapsed Great Uncle Winchester's secretary remained in the study, working long into the night, ferreting away at his sedentary task, seemingly fully immersed in it. Finally the clock struck ten, despite all her trying to keep her eyes open, Dotty was overtaken by sleep, curled up with Geoff in the corridor, head leant against the lamp table. The night's waiting game, for that is what it had become, for Dotty had been lost.

Dotty awoke with a start as the clock struck one. Realising immediately that Strake was gone, she made an effort to stand, forgetting that she was still wearing her skates and found her legs less than compliant in her bid to become upright. Staggering to her feet, and then at once to the closed study door, Dotty rattled the door handle. She groaned, realising with frustration that the door was locked. It was no use; she was never going to get in there whilst Strake was around. She needed to find another way in.

With Geoff padding along beside her, feeling tired and despondent Dotty went up to bed, stopping off on the way to grab the bowl of dessert from the fridge by way of consolation prize. Reaching her bedroom, she felt around the door frame with one hand for the light, jam roly poly carefully tucked under her other arm, and flicked on the switch.

The bowl clattered to the floor, the impact splattering cold custard everywhere, the sticky dessert in contrast keeping the shattered bowl more or less together, albeit now in pieces. Dotty stared in horror at her room. It had been ransacked. Books lay open all over the floor; the covers had been torn from the bed, the mattress overturned; every drawer lay open and emptied. Someone had been searching for the Key. Slowly the cold realisation dawned upon her. It must have been Strake!

Dotty couldn't believe it. All the while she had been watching and waiting for Strake in the corridor, Strake had also been waiting for her. Seemingly engrossed in his work but biding his time, Strake had been waiting for her to become tired: to sleep. Away from her bedroom, away from the place where the Calendar House Key was safely hidden, so that he could go in search of it undisturbed. Dotty smiled grimly. Strake must have overheard her telling Pip that she had hidden it in her bedroom. The one small comfort in all this was that he could not have found it of course; not here at least: for the locket was not hidden in Dotty's bedroom. Well, not in this bedroom, anyway.

All at once Dotty felt sick. Mam's Playroom! What if he had looked there too? Could he have had time? Surely he must have. Panic–stricken, Dotty turned, scrabbling forwards, her legs failing her as she skated helter-skelter through the house, Geoff in dogged pursuit; onwards, onwards along the vast empty hallway and up the rickety back stairs, until she reached it. Oh please, please let Mam's Playroom be safe! Flinging open the heavy wooden door at the top of the stairs she snapped on the light, the breath tight in her lungs.

All was quiet. Everything lay as it should be: undisturbed; peaceful.

Dotty skated across the room to the doll's house. Fearful that Strake should still be spying on her, she searched the room for signs of him. Seeing nothing, she closed the playroom door and double checked that the drapes were firmly closed across the window. Sinking to her knees, Dotty reached into the Doll's house, to the place where she had hidden the locket. And there it was still: tucked safely under the bed in the tiny doll's house replica of her bedroom.

Relief flooded over her. "Oh thank goodness! I don't know what I would have done if..." Dotty clutched the locket to her. "Oh you're a troublesome thing!" she laughed in spite of herself.

To the exhausted Dotty, the big old nursery rocking chair in the corner suddenly looked exceedingly inviting. Still cradling the locket in one arm (she didn't dare put it round her neck, in case she unleashed some of the magic that had alerted Porguss and Poachling to its presence in the house), Dotty clambered awkwardly onto the rocking chair, roller blades still strapped to her, and pulled the chequered woollen blanket over her tired limbs.

Geoff settled protectively at her feet. Dotty shivered, not from the cold, but from the remnants of adrenalin that had torn through her body at the thought of the locket's discovery. For a moment fear threatened to rob her of sleep, but Dotty's exhaustion was greater still and in moments she found herself slipping helter-skelter into a dead and dreamless slumber.

When Dotty awoke it was morning. Her first instinct was to search for the locket, but she didn't have to look far, as it was still grasped firmly in her hand, the chain wound tightly around her closed fist. Swinging her legs down heavily from the great old chair her booted feet hit a large furry obstacle on the floor beneath her. Geoff yelped as his muzzle came into close contact with Dotty's left roller blade. "Sorry, Geoff," she apologised, ruffling Geoff's head and giving his ears a scratch.

"I forgot you were there." Geoff looked suitably hurt, but enjoyed the fuss anyway. "Come on. We'd better get back to my room," Dotty yawned. "We need to tell Pip what has happened. And tidy up the mess, too."

Dotty felt glum. She didn't like tidying up at the best of times, and in these circumstances least of all. On the up side, she was still wearing her roller blades from last night, so she would get there that much quicker than she otherwise would have done. As she neared her bedroom, she saw the mess of the smashed crockery in the bedroom doorway and her heart sank. She had forgotten just how bad it was and in the daylight things looked even worse than they had done the night before. What a mess.

Not knowing quite where to start, Dotty picked up the broken pudding bowl as best she could, scooping the mess of broken china and jam roly poly into the waste paper basket beside her bed. Geoff obligingly began to lick the splattered custard up off the floor. "Watch out, Geoff, there might be broken china mixed in with that," she warned. Geoff wasn't listening.

Dotty stuffed a couple of armfuls of clothes back into open drawers and sighed. This was going to take forever. In need of a diversion, she waded across the mess on the bedroom floor and leant across to the hearth, pressing the servants' bell. In an instant, there was a scritch and a scratch and a whoosh and a sploosh and Pip came tumbling down the chimney.

"At your service, Miss," Pip announced with a grin. "Cor blimey, Miss Dotty, you need to tidy your room. A fella could hurt himself, tripping up over this lot." Pip picked through the debris that lay on the hearth as he spoke, careful not to tread on anything. "Say, are you alright?"

"Well no not exactly," Dotty replied. "In fact, not at all. I think you'd better have a seat."

Pip sat quiet for once whilst he listened without interruption to Dotty's account of the events of the night before. "So, you see," Dotty concluded "I do think we can still make the plan work, albeit with a few tweaks, and with your help of course."

When she had finished Pip rose to his feet, looking suddenly weary. "For my part, Miss Dotty, it would be my honour to help you in any way that I can." He frowned, "the magick you speak of is beyond a simple sweep like me, I'm afraid, but I may be able to call in a couple of favours and get you what you ask for. I'll have to tell the Sweeps' Council, of course," he said. "They won't be happy, but hopefully if I explain it to them they will see that it's the only way."

"Right," said Dotty. "We're all set then. You let me know about the magick and I'll speak to Sylv. And in the meantime I'd better tidy up this room before Gobby sees it and has a pink fit." Dotty grimaced.

"Do you want some help?" ventured Pip.

"No, thanks all the same, Pip," chuckled Dotty. "No offence but you'd just make everything dirty as well as messy!" she grinned, "Although you could just help me to get this mattress back onto the bed before you go. I wouldn't have credited Strake with so much strength. He looks like he'd snap in a storm."

*

After several hours and a couple of snack breaks (for Geoff more than Dotty) finally Dotty's bedroom looked almost presentable again and she was able to sit down on her bed and give Sylv a call.

"Sylv, I know you don't believe me but you've gotta trust me on this one, okay? You're the only one I can rely on. We really need you for the plan to work."

"Okay, okay." Sylv was taking some persuading. "Well I still thinks you're bonkers Dot but if it means that much to you I'm in."

Dotty squealed with excitement. "Oh Sylv, that's brilliant. Thank you so much; I'm so grateful. And I promise you, I'm not crazy! Now then, just remember," Dotty was serious for a moment. "Pip will be with you tomorrow at five o'clock, after it gets dark. Just try not to freak out when you see him, alright?"

"And why would I do that? He hasn't got two heads as well has he, this sweep friend of yours?" Sylv teased.

"No, nothing like that," replied Dotty. She just hoped Sylv took the boy appearing in her chimney place rather better than Dotty herself had. Knowing Sylv as she did, she seriously doubted it.

"Alright, then. I'll speak to you tonight Dot."

"Just let me know when you've got the package, okay?" Dotty fussed.

"Yes, yes. Don't worry about it. I've got it covered." Sylv signed off.

"Well that's it then." Dotty turned to the ever-present Geoff. "All we have to do now, boy, is wait."

Chapter 12

A Visit to Cardiff

In which Dotty sends a package to Sylv and Strake gets his comeuppance

There suddenly seemed to be so much to do. Dotty sat down at the writing desk in her bedroom and took out a sheet of paper and a pen. A plate of ham sandwiches and half a dozen ripe cherry tomatoes sat piled up on a plate beside her. The freshly baked ham was still warm and the smell of that, combined with the home baked white crusty farmhouse bread that enveloped it, was making her stomach rumble. Geoff obviously felt the same as he was making a point of looking at Dotty with his best doe-eyes, mouth salivating wildly. She took a bite of one of the sandwiches and threw Geoff a tomato.

"Dear Sylv..." she wrote.

Dotty finished chewing her mouthful of sandwich and took to gnawing her pen for concentration instead. She had to get this finished before Pip arrived.

Geoff clearly didn't like the tomato, but in the absence of the coveted sandwich made a valiant attempt to eat it anyway, rolling it around his mouth with a look of sheer disgust on his face and then spitting it onto the carpet when he could bear it no longer. Tomato pips stuck in the fur around his mouth. He whined a little and looked at Dotty, hoping for a reprieve, but Dotty was enjoying the baked ham far too much to give any away. Geoff harrumphed despondently and picked up the disgorged and now rather fluff-ridden tomato off the carpet for another munch.

Dotty alternately took bites of the sandwiches and chewed the end of her pen while she thought. Pip would be (quite literally) dropping in later to collect it and the letter had to be ready for him when he arrived so that he could take it to Sylv. She must think.

"...Please find enclosed in this package the item we talked about last night. Keep it safe until we meet again.

Chapter 12

Lots of love
Dotty xxx"

Satisfied with her work, Dotty folded the letter neatly into four and placed it in the envelope together with its small circular enclosure. She moistened the flap of the envelope with her tongue, sticking it down carefully to make sure it would hold its contents tight. Then as an added safety measure she took out her sticker book and stuck a big round sticker on the back, across the join of the envelope. The sticker read 'keep out!' which Dotty thought appropriate.

As Dotty sat admiring her work the tell-tale smell of soot wafted under her nose. Dotty knew immediately that Pip was on his way. Almost at once there came the familiar *scritch-scratch-thud* of her friend's arrival as Pip clattered down the chimney and into her bedroom.

"Pip, I've been worried," Dotty fussed. "Is everything okay? Did you manage to speak to the Sweeps' Council? Have they given you their answer?"

"Never fear, Miss Dotty, I have it all in hand" said Pip with his usual cheerfulness. "I've spoken to the Council and its good news. They are on board with the plan but they have given me strict instructions that if our mission fails the locket must be destroyed."

"Destroyed? I didn't even know it could be destroyed!" exclaimed Dotty.

"Oh it's easy enough to do, Miss," Pip explained. "You just have to break the seal that contains the sweep's kiss and set the magick free. In the case of your mother's key we would just need to break the glass frame in the back of the locket."

"Fair enough then. Although it does seem a shame," Dotty remarked. "To break it, I mean. I hope it's not necessary."

"Me too," agreed Pip. "Me too. But it won't come to that, I'm certain. We just have to make sure that we time everything just right, that's all." Dotty nodded, unsure if Pip was trying to reassure herself or him.

"Say, you don't know who the picture is of, do you, Pip?" asked Dotty, taking her opportunity. "The picture of the boy in the locket, I mean."

"Oh that'll be the sweep who made the key," replied Pip. "It usually is."

"I see," said Dotty. "But who is that? Do you know who it is that made this one?" she questioned. "Do you recognise the boy on the back?"

"I'm afraid not," replied Pip. "It's before my time, unfortunately."

Dotty was disappointed. "That's such a shame. I'd have loved to know who it was. Anyway, down to business." Dotty recognised that now wasn't the time to labour the point.

"Here's the package for Sylv." Dotty handed over the envelope to Pip. "Guard it with your life!" she said, only half joking. "And try not to scare Sylv to death when you come down the chimney."

"Right you are, Miss Dotty," laughed Pip. "I'll do my best, Scout's honour." Pip turned to go. Then, stopping himself, he turned back to Dotty. "I nearly forgot, Miss." Pip proffered something to her, hand outstretched. "I have something for you too."

Dotty glanced quizzically at the small unassuming object in Pip's hand. It looked like an old butterfly chrysalis, dry and papery, strung on a fine gossamer thread.

"It's that little piece of faerie magick we talked about," Pip explained. "Now take good care of it, d'you hear? I had to pull some serious favours to get one of those.

"Thanks, Pip." Dotty put out her hand to take it from him. As she did so, Pip grabbed her hand in his, taking it firmly in his grasp.

"Good luck, Dotty," he said with meaning. Dotty took the chrysalis, pulling her hand away from his a little awkwardly. She blushed. Her hand tingled slightly.

"You'd better go." Dotty put the chrysalis safely in her pocket to use later.

Pip did not reply, but leaving her one of his winning smiles he whizzed back off up the chimney, the letter sticking out of his pocket.

A loud bell broke Dotty from her reverie. It was the front door. No one ever used the front door! Dotty ran to the main staircase and hung over the bannister. She saw Gobby hurrying to the door, dusting flour from her hands as she walked. It was a taxi driver. "Taxi to the train Station for Mr Strake," the man announced.

"I didn't know Mr Strake was due to travel," offered the cook by way of answer. "I'll go see if I can fetch him for you." And off she tripped on her disconcertingly light feet to find him.

Dotty watched and waited. Moments later Strake came hurrying into the hallway, pulling on a slim black overcoat over his deformed frame. Dotty noticed his hair seemed out of place, and he appeared to be sweating. "Bleugh!" Dotty exclaimed involuntarily. He really was a vile creature. She put her hand over her mouth to shush herself. She couldn't afford to have any more outbursts. She didn't want to be seen.

Gobby scampered along behind Strake, fussing after him as she went, and talking incessantly. The running commentary was actually quite helpful for once, and Dotty listened intently.

"Now, Mr Strake, where is it that you are going? There is nothing in the diary. What about food?" (Of course this was the all-important question for Gobby). "I could have made you a packed lunch for the train. Will you be home late? Shall I make you supper? I could leave you a ploughman's and a slice of cake in the larder in case you are peckish when you return."

Gobby needed to breathe soon; she was starting to go purple. "Yes, that's what I'll do. I have some lovely mature cheddar and I'll put on a couple of pickled onions and an apple and a slice of baked ham." Gobby prattled on, happy now that she was providing. "And I've a nice piece of coconut crumble cake that I can leave out for you. That should suffice, shouldn't it? Say, what time did you say you would be returning?"

Gobby's preoccupation with feeding Strake was rendered all the more amusing by the fact that it was quite clear to Dotty that Great Uncle Winchester's emaciated private secretary hadn't eaten in at least a hundred years. She let slip a small giggle. Strake looked up sharply, his beady eyes focused in Dotty's direction. Dotty threw herself into the shadows on the landing. She hoped he hadn't seen her. He appeared not to have and turned towards the front door.

At this point the taxi driver had obviously tired of Gobby's diatribe and came to Strake's rescue, asking "You're getting the Cardiff train aren't you, Sir? We're going to have to get a move on if you want to catch the eleven thirty, begging your pardon, Madam." The taxi driver held open the rear passenger door of the cab for his ride. As he went out the door

Dotty looked out past him onto the driveway. There were half a dozen jackdaws out on the driveway, hopping about, as if they were watching the spectacle. *Strange,* thought Dotty. Perhaps Gobby had thrown some crumbs out for them. But she usually did that out the back door, not the front.

"Cardiff?" asked Gobby. "That's an awfully long way to go and be back in time for supper."

Strake shot the taxi driver a look that clearly said he didn't want his business in Cardiff to be known and then neatly glided out of the doorway and into the waiting taxi. "You must be mistaken, man," retorted Strake, addressing the taxi driver. "I am catching the London train."

He turned to Gobby. "Good morning, Madam," he said with finality. And then the taxi was gone.

Gobby closed the front door and wandered back off towards the kitchen, muttering to herself about journeys and timings and food preparation, now that she no longer had an audience. Dotty picked herself up from the floor and raced back to her bedroom. She had to speak to Pip again.

"Pip! *PIIIP!*" Dotty yelled, prodding at the fireplace bell. After a few moments a faraway voice echoed down the chimney.

"I'm indisposed at the moment, Miss. Can you tell me what it is?"

Feeling a bit daft, Dotty shouted back up the chimney. "Pip, we were right! Strake has been listening to our conversations. He's on his way to

Chapter 12

Cardiff to try and intercept the package. Just be careful, okay?"

"Right you are, Miss Dotty," came the echoey reply.

Dotty sat back, but her thoughts were fraught with worry for Sylv. She hoped Sylv would be okay. She didn't like the thought of her best friend being cornered by the venomous Strake. Dotty was very tempted to call Sylv; to warn her of the danger. But there was no need, she reminded herself. Pip would be with her, and Pip could handle anything. In any case, she couldn't risk talking to Sylv over Skype. If Strake had been listening in then others could be too. She just couldn't take the chance. Everything would be fine, Dotty was sure. She just had to be patient and let the plan take its course.

But it was a nail biting afternoon, nonetheless. Dotty sat and clock watched, listening to the chimes of the grandfather clock in the hallway, waiting for it to finally strike five.

*

In Cardiff, Sylv was doing much the same. In a desperate attempt to pass the time she excavated a 'painting by numbers' kit from under her bed that she had been given for her birthday, and started to do that. Sylv struggled to concentrate. She scrutinised the picture. Thinking about it she was pretty sure Little Red Riding Hood's cloak shouldn't be blue. She frowned at the number key. Ah, that was it: it was a 13, not an 18 she should have been reading. Her patience coming to an abrupt halt, Sylv cast the canvas aside in disgust. "I'll sort that out later," she grouched.

Sylv looked at her watch. It was a quarter to five. "Fifteen minutes," she told herself. "He should be here in fifteen minutes."

"I can't believe I'm sitting here in my bedroom like a lemon waiting for my best friend's imaginary friend to arrive," she complained to herself.

"You don't look much like a lemon to me," a voice came from the fireplace. "Say, isn't that supposed to be Little *Red* Riding Hood?"

Sylv turned to see a scruffy, dirty little boy standing in the bedroom fireplace. She screamed.

As Dotty had anticipated it took Pip quite a while to calm Sylv down, but he got there eventually with his winning smile and a bit of cheeky chimney sweep charm. With the package safely handed over Pip was about to take his leave when the doorbell rang. It was one of those battery operated doorbells that plays a really rubbish tune when you ring it. *Nee-nah-nah-nah-nah tiddle pom,* it went.

"Oh, hang on a minute, Pip," said Sylv. "I'd better get that. Dad said he was expecting a parcel today. I'll be in no end of trouble if I don't sign for it." The doorbell went again: *nee-nah-nah-nah-nah tiddle pom.*

Chapter 12

"Crikey, they're impatient," moaned Sylv, dropping Dotty's letter on the bed and heading for the stairs. "Now, don't go disappearing back off up that chimney, will you," she instructed Pip.

"Blimey," exclaimed Pip. "I know why you and Miss Dotty are such good friends," he complained good naturedly, "you're as bossy as each other!" He grinned after her. Sylv stuck her tongue out at him and ran down the stairs. She could see why Dotty liked Pip. The three of them were going to make a great team.

Pip listened as Sylv opened the door. He heard a man's voice: high pitched and whining. The hairs on the back of his neck stood up. Instinct told him that this wasn't Parcel Force. Pip dithered for a moment. He wasn't sure what to do. Should he go downstairs or not? But before he could make a decision Sylv reappeared at the bedroom door accompanied by a sinister looking man, impossibly thin, with a stoop and an altogether inhuman air about him. It was Strake.

Strake's hand gripped Sylv's shoulder tightly. For once, Pip's cheeky smile was gone. "Hey, let go of her," he snarled.

Sylv was wide-eyed, her breathing quick and shallow. She was scared now, truly scared. She did not like this man, not one little bit. She didn't want to be a part of Dotty's adventure any more.

It had stopped being fun now. She just wanted it to end.

"Give me the letter," dictated Strake to Pip, his voice full of menace.

"And don't try to be clever about it, or I have a couple of friends who I am sure would be very pleased to employ a new chimney boy…or girl." He squeezed Sylv's shoulder. Sylv began to cry.

Not to be intimidated, Pip puffed his chest out bravely, "I always knew you was no gentleman," spat Pip. "Just look at you, manhandling a young lady like that. If you had an ounce of humanity in you, you would know just how shameful your behaviour was." Pip squared up to Strake, who towered over him. "Why Mr Winchester ever employed you I have no idea," Pip continued. "Now, we ain't giving you anything until you let Miss Sylvia go, so hop to it." Pip crossed his arms and stared Strake straight in the eye, his expectations made clear.

Strake recoiled visibly at the mention of his employer, looking momentarily unsure. Then, regaining his composure, he slowly stretched out a spidery hand towards the boy, the other still firmly on Sylv's shoulder.

"Just give me what I came for and I will release the girl," he offered. "I *promise*," he leered, a sinister smile playing on his lips. Pip took a deep breath. He knew he could not trust this man but what other choice did he have? He reached over to the bed and picked up the package.

"No!" screamed Sylv. "Dotty told us not to! Don't give it to him, Pip!" The little sweep looked

Chapter 12

at Sylv, his face full of regret. "We don't have a choice Miss Sylvia. I can't let him take you. You don't know how horrible it is up those chimneys. You'd be worse than lost." Pip broke Sylv's gaze "I'm sorry," he whispered, and handed Strake the letter.

Strake let go of Sylv and grabbed the package in both hands, holding it aloft. Sylv ran to Pip, who ushered her behind him protectively.

"I'VE GOT IT," he shrieked triumphantly. **"I'VE FINALLY GOT IT!"** Strake laughed maniacally, gleefully. His long sharp fingers tore at the envelope, ripping Dotty's 'Keep Out' sticker in two. Pip and Sylv watched in fearful anticipation as Strake shook the packet, emptying the contents into the palm of his hand.

All at once Strake's rapture turned into rage. He stared for a moment in disbelief at the small circular object that now lay in his hand. It wasn't Dotty's locket as he had expected: it wasn't the missing Calendar House Key. Instead Strake found himself staring at one of Great Uncle Winchester's mint humbugs: striped sticky sweet perfection and utterly harmless.

Such was Strake's fury that he hopped from foot to foot, a long thin streak of anger looking for an outlet. The gangly man threw the offending piece of confection to the floor, trying to stamp it into oblivion, but the sweet simply stuck to the sole of his pointed leather shoe, enraging him yet further as he tried to shake it off.

"Wow look at that, Pip, Mr Creepy's doing the angry dance," Sylv mocked, finding her confidence at last.

Strake turned, his steely gaze alighting on the source of his humiliation, a look of pure hatred in his eyes. *Uh oh*, thought Pip. *This is going to get nasty.*

But at that moment Sylv's dad returned home: the unwitting cavalry come to save the day. "Hiya, love," he called out from downstairs. The front door banged shut. "Did my parcel arrive?" Sylv beamed triumphantly. Good old Dad! "Hiya, Dad," she called back, eyes never leaving Strake. "No, nothing yet I'm afraid." Sylv glared at the intruder, daring him to remain there: to be caught.

Beaten, Strake turned on his heel and fled through the open bedroom window.

Chapter 13

Dotty Takes Flight

In which Dotty flees from Porguss and Poachling

It was twenty-five to six. Pip came tumbling helter-skelter down the Calendar House chimneys and onto Dotty's hearth. He stood for a moment, head down, hands on knees, catching his breath.

Dotty leapt down from the bed. "Come on!" she urged him, unable to bear the suspense. "Tell me! What happened? Are you okay? Is Sylv okay? Did Strake take the bait?"

Pip looked up, still breathing heavily, grinning all over his face. "Well your friend's a barrel of laughs, that's for sure," he chortled. "I can see why you two are as thick as thieves."

Dotty heaved a sigh of relief. "But she's okay though, isn't she, Pip? Sylv's going to be okay on her own?"

"Yes she'll be fine. She's full of spirit that one! Anyway her dad's home: no-one will bother her now."

Reassured as to her friend's safety, Dotty moved on. "So spill the beans then. What happened with Strake? I assume he turned up?"

"Oh you should have seen it, Miss Dotty. He arrived at the house just as we expected, right on cue, looking for the Key," Pip recounted. "And he was so, *so* furious when he realised it was just a sticky old sweet that you had sent Miss Sylvia and not the locket at all. He nearly went mad with rage," Pip laughed at the memory. "Miss Sylvia was brilliant. She wound him up good and proper. I honestly thought Strake was going to explode at one point."

Dotty chuckled. "I'm sorry to have missed that; it sounds like it made awesome watching."

"It was, it really was, Miss Dotty." Pip paused, still catching his breath "Right," he wheezed, "we need to get moving. I can give you all the details later. Strake will be sending a message to Porguss and Poachling as we speak. There's no time to lose."

"What about Strake, though?" Everything to do with that man made Dotty nervous. "Surely he'll be making his way back here?"

"Yes, but it'll take another four hours on the train, plus an hour's taxi ride from the station. By the time he gets here if everything goes according to plan it will all be over." Pip was all business now. "Okay, so you know what you're doing?"

"Yes," said Dotty in a small voice. "But, oh, Pip, I'm scared!" she shivered, suddenly feeling the cold in the room.

"Don't worry, Miss Dotty, you'll be fine. Just do everything exactly like we said and remember to stand your ground. I'll be waiting for you on the other side." Pip gave Dotty a wink. "We're counting on you, Miss Dotty. We're all counting on you." And in an instant Pip was gone.

Dotty sat herself back down on her bed. *Right this is it!* she thought and, reaching under her pillow, pulled out her mum's locket. She took a deep breath and waited. For a while, all was quiet. Dotty turned the locket over in her hand; over and again, waiting, waiting. She held the locket tight, the responsibility of it weighing heavily upon her.

Suddenly, from out of nowhere Dotty thought she heard a tap at the window. *Tap!* it went. *Tap, tap, tap!* Dotty ran across to the blind, peering through a chink in the curtain. It had been dark for a couple of hours now. Straining to focus she stared hard into the blackness. *Tap, tap.* The blackness moved. Recoiling, Dotty realised she was not staring into the dark at all; rather she was staring *at* something dark. It was a jackdaw.

Slowly she drew back the blind. In horror Dotty saw that this was not just one jackdaw: it was a *whole row* of jackdaws, all huddled together on the window ledge, vying for a view through the gap between the curtain edges. Even as she watched another landed, struggling for space on the sill. The birds observed her with black beady eyes, taking it in turns to peck at the glass. *Tap. Tap, TAP, TAP!* They were on to her. Dotty felt sick.

From somewhere behind her Dotty became aware of an unnatural breeze stirring. she spun around quickly. The breeze was coming from the fireplace. All at once the birds stopped tapping, their gaze turning to the chimney. Their beetle-y little eyes focused together on the grate. For a moment Dotty stood, fear rooting her to the spot. Then from out of the darkness a twin voice echoed in unison: "WE'RE COMING TO GET YOU!" it chorused.

There was a crunch and a grind as the top of the chimney breast began to bulge. The plasterwork splintered. Porguss and Poachling were making their descent. Suddenly the jackdaws sprang into action, their tapping turning to pecking and clawing at the window pane, ever more frantic. They were trying to get in, to greet their masters. The window pane cracked. At any moment they would break the glass. There was no time now to watch the spectacle unfold. There was nothing for it. Dotty had to run.

Chapter 13

Dotty cursed herself for not having worn her roller blades. *All that time waiting,* she scolded herself, *and you didn't even prepare properly. You could have been so much faster.* But there was no time for regrets now. She would just have to make do with feet instead of wheels. She tore through the house at top speed, heading for the pretty wallpapered sitting room, the room she liked to refer to as the 'Bird Room'. The quickest route to the bird room and its glass house with doors out onto the garden was down the main staircase and through the grand hallway. Dotty hurtled down the marble steps, hand skimming the polished handrail as she went. *Perhaps the skates wouldn't have been such a great idea,* she concluded.

Racing through the hallway Dotty finally reached her destination. She slammed the heavy oak door of the Bird Room behind her and leant against it for a second, surveying the room for unwanted company. If only the door had a lock! Still, at least she was alone for the moment…or was she? The thick curtains that covered the French doors into the glass house had not been closed for the night and, as Dotty switched on a side lamp to light the room, she spotted movement beyond the glass. She squinted. The glass house was dark and full of shadow and…oh no! It was full of birds! Someone must have left the air vents open in the glass roof and the jackdaws had found their way in. There were hundreds of them: covering plants and wicker chairs and pink granite table tops, cawing and scratching and waiting. *Oh my goodness!* thought Dotty. Perhaps this had not been the best room to escape to after all. As she surveyed the scene one of the jackdaws noticed her presence in the room and hopped over to the glass. *Tap. Tap, tap, tap!* It wouldn't be long before they were all at it and then the Bird Room really would become a 'bird room' in quite the most literal sense!

Dotty stood pondering for a moment what to do. But it was a moment too long. As she paused for thought the heavy brass door knob rattled, and then began slowly to turn on its axis. The hinges of the great old door squeaked a greeting as the Bird Room door began to open. The door swung wide, revealing as it did so in all their gruesome splendour the odious forms of Porguss and Poachling. Their fat bodies filled every inch of the door frame as they leered and sneered at her in all their hideous glory. Dotty was trapped!

On witnessing their masters' arrival, one by one the jackdaws started making their way towards the French doors that formed the thin glass division between the Bird Room and the glass house beyond. The first bird croaked its master a greeting. Dotty's eyes flitted, horrified, between the approaching birds and their masters. "Good evening, Mistress." Porguss oozed towards Dotty. "We'll be taking that locket now, thanking you kindly." Porguss held out an impossibly chubby and unpleasantly dirty hand.

Chapter 13

Dotty clutched the locket tightly. "No you won't," she retorted, jutting out her chin. The jackdaws had begun pecking at the glass; pecking and croaking, calling to their masters. Dotty drew herself up straight, defiant. Her lip trembled slightly.

"Oh come now, Mistress," Porguss continued in her most persuasive tone, her voice supported with a renewed chorus of tapping and cawing. "You know this simply won't do. We shall have our locket one way or another." She smiled her deadliest smile, sharp little teeth prominent in the lamplight. "Why make things difficult for yourself?" she cajoled.

"You're not having it," Dotty insisted. "It's not yours." Indignation welled within her. "The locket belonged to my mother and now it belongs to me. You two are nothing but common *thieves*!" The squawking of the jackdaws was rising to a din.

Now it was Poachling's turn to interject. "Listen to me, you little wretch," he menaced. "We have made it our business to have the Key, and have it we shall" he growled. "You have no knowledge of the business of which you speak, and you would do well not to meddle in the business of others." As Poachling spoke he edged forwards, silent, slithering, gliding almost. Dotty backed away. "I have warned you that it would not end well for you if you were not forthcoming with the item we seek and you have chosen not to heed my advice." The jackdaws croaked and screeched, their awful accompaniment reaching a crescendo. "And now look at you," he sneered. "All backed up and no place to go."

Dotty stopped dead. Poachling's face lit up: pure evil written on his features. Dotty was standing with her back to the hearth. She could back away no further and, with both the room exits covered, there was nowhere else to go. Dotty was terrified. *Remember what Pip said* she told herself. *You can do it Dotty Parsons. Just hold your ground!* Dotty stood quite still, matching Poachling's deadly stare with her own. Slowly, steadily, she placed the chain of the locket around her neck, the locket still held tightly in the palm of her hand. A crackle of electricity buzzed in the air. Fearful now, she glanced back towards the open fireplace.

"Where do you think you are you going, Mistress?" Porguss snaked forward. "If you have ideas of escape I should counsel you not to trouble yourself. If I were you I would stay right where you are. Your efforts will be pointless. There's nowhere to run, you know; nowhere you can hide." Dotty quaked, every fibre of her being struggling to keep it together. She glanced at the fire grate again.

"Oh and if you are thinking of chimney hopping, I wouldn't," Porguss continued. "Once you enter the chimneys you and your trinket will know no safe harbour from us." Porguss smiled an evil smile. "There are many who serve us. We will follow you wherever you go. We will find you and catch you…"

"And make you a sweep!" Poachling interrupted his counterpart once more, a flicker of delight crossing his face at the thought of Dotty's imminent demise. The jackdaws clamoured and bayed at the glass, their clawing and pecking relentless. The din was almost unbearable. Dotty sensed that the idea of her being enslaved and at their masters' whim and at the sharp end of a sweep's broom was pleasing these malevolent birds.

"Oh yes, Mistress," Porguss gleefully continued the line of threat. "It is not an occupation I would recommend you." She spoke, voice raised above the crowing of the jackdaws. "Indeed, I am certain you would find it most disagreeable." Poachling leered at Dotty, nodding in assent at his twin.

"Do you know what it is like, Mistress, the life of a sweep?" Porguss continued. "A life of never-ending darkness, and toil and soot. The loneliness and the fear are said to be almost unbearable, or so they say, isn't that right dearest brother?" The pair advanced toward Dotty, almost within reach of the locket around her neck. "Now, you wouldn't want that, would you, Mistress?" They were tantalizingly close now; just one swipe and the locket would be theirs…

There was an almighty crash as the glass in the French doors finally gave way. A screaming torrent of jackdaws flooded into the room, reducing the dim light into feathery darkness as they wheeled and circled against their paper counterparts on the wallpaper. For a split second Porguss and Poachling were out of sight as the cloud of birds filed in between them and the terrified Dotty.

"I'll take my chances," Dotty whispered, and stepped backwards into the fireplace.

Chapter 14

Up the Chimney, Down the Chimney

In which Dotty chimney hops and the rogue sweeps get stuck in the chimney

It all seemed to happen so much more quickly than it had the last time Dotty had stepped into a fireplace with the locket around her neck. Maybe it was because this time she knew exactly where she wanted to go. In any event there was no mistaking the unnatural electricity-charged wind that whipped around her, lifting her up off her feet and carrying her into the air. There was a crackle of energy and all of a sudden she was flying, or rather she was not flying exactly; moreover she was being propelled upwards, at break-neck speed, through the labyrinth of vertical tunnels that formed the chimneys of the Calendar House.

Bright sparks bounced around the chimney, lighting her path as she went, her clothes skimming the brick work, worn smooth from centuries of use. Dotty felt like a shot being fired out of a gun; or a cork out of champagne; or one of those daredevil circus acts being expelled out of a giant cannon; except Dotty was painfully aware that she wasn't wearing a crash helmet. But even as quickly as she tried to get used to being fired headlong into oblivion, she abruptly changed direction, now flying feet first in a downwards spiral towards the ground. Dotty was heading into land, to her final destination: Mam's Playroom.

As Dotty made her descent suddenly she became aware of the chimney starting to narrow. She slowed, her clothes beginning to brush the walls where before they had just skimmed them. She must be getting close to the playroom now: close to the flue that linked the playroom stove to the chimney. The flue was far too narrow for a girl even of Dotty's size to travel. She was going to get stuck! As her downward pace began to slacken she heard the unmistakable caw of a jackdaw above her. *Caw! Croak croak caw!* it went. One of the awful birds must have followed her up the chimney. In fact, now she listened she was pretty sure it was more than one.

Chapter 14

Dotty wondered if Porguss and Poachling were in pursuit behind them. But she had no time to consider that now; she had more pressing matters to attend to, like the chimney pressing in on her! Quickly she fished in her pocket. For a moment she didn't find what she was looking for and she thought she must have lost it during her flight.

Her hand blindly searched the small square of fabric, trying to find its cargo. In her efforts Dotty scraped her elbow on the brickwork as she went round a corner "Ouch!" she exclaimed. Things were getting pretty tight in here! And then she felt it under her fingers. The small papery chrysalis Pip had given to her: the faerie charm on its gossamer thread.

Awkwardly, Dotty slipped the chrysalis around her neck, careful not to scrape any more extremities as she did so. The chrysalis settled next to the locket. There was a little spark as the two magical trinkets met one another: as if they were exchanging a magical greeting of sorts.

Dotty's nose was now within an inch of the soot-covered passage. Closing her eyes, she clasped the locket and the chrysalis together in her hand and quietly whispered to them the words that Pip had told her. "Magick be mine; magick be mine!" The chrysalis all at once began to glow. Dotty released it from her grasp and the chrysalis lit the chimney with a greenish light, allowing her to see the way. Suddenly as she travelled she could see the bricks moving below her; twisting, turning, realigning themselves to create an altogether bigger pathway through the chimney. The eerie light changed from green to blue. Dotty could see the top of the playroom range below her. *Oh please let it work!*

Dotty watched amazed as the faerie charm wrought its magick, the fireplace below changing before her eyes, morphing into something else: something from an older time: a big, dark, open fireplace. Dotty could feel its age as she travelled through it, as if the fireplace had a signature all of its own. She smelled the aroma of burnt wood: ancient pine. There was no coal here. This must have been the fireplace that had been here at the Calendar House before the room had become a playroom; Mam's Playroom.

And then she was landing. Before Dotty knew it her feet were touching the ground again; hitting the old earthy hearth. She fell forwards, stumbling as if landing after jumping off a high wall. Such was the force with which she fell that she skidded and, struggling to retain her balance, finally halted herself within a few steps, narrowly avoiding a crash landing into the doll's house. Dotty coughed and spluttered, fighting to catch her breath as Pip always did when he landed.

Dotty's head spun. It felt like the feeling she always had after getting off the roundabout in the playground up the road from her house in Cardiff. What a ride! If Alton Towers had one of these they'd make a fortune, she was certain. Personally Dotty wasn't too keen on roundabouts or pirate ships as they had a tendency to make her queasy. Sylv on the other hand was going to *love* this, of that she was quite sure. Dotty couldn't wait to tell her all about it. But for the moment she must keep her excitement in check. There was still work to do here.

Dotty turned back towards the now open hearth. The ancient fireplace still glowed, its surround flickering slightly, like a television that wasn't quite tuned in fully, giving the old fireplace an air of fragility: of unreality. Dotty wondered how long the magick would hold. As she watched a cawing and a croaking echoed in the chimney breast and a jackdaw bowled out of the fireplace, it too coughing and spluttering, feathers shedding in all directions. The bird righted itself, shook its head as if to clear it and then hopped across the room, finally alighting on one of the chimneys of the dolls' house. It eyed Dotty with seeming satisfaction. It had fulfilled its duty: following its quarry to her resting place.

Dotty was frightened that it would attack her, but the bird did nothing further for the moment, simply watching her with quizzical interest. "Shoo!" Dotty flapped her arms at the bird, trying to get it to move. "Get on with you, *shoo!*"

The jackdaw didn't move. It just held her gaze steadily, unafraid. It was waiting for instructions from its masters. They must be on their way. Ignoring the immoveable bird, Dotty turned her attention to the fire. The sound of multiple cawings and wheezings rumbled around the fire opening. There were more jackdaws in pursuit.

Dotty was scared at the thought of being faced with the jackdaws, loose in the playroom in their numbers, but for now they were no more than an unpleasant distraction; an irritation to be ignored whilst she waited for the real threat to reveal itself: the twin threat of the rogue sweeps that meant to steal the locket and enslave her forever in the chimneys. She stood her ground, waiting as another two jackdaws flew out of the chimney, hopping onto one arm of the rocking chair. Dotty was beginning to feel outnumbered. But then it came: the noise she had been waiting for - the sound of Porguss and Poachling's approach.

There was nothing stealthy about their descent. They shouted as they came. "*WheeeeeeeeEEEE!*" they sang in unison. They were clearly enjoying themselves. "We're right bee-*hind* you!" Porguss taunted. "Thank you for making your capture *so* enjoyable," sneered Poachling. Their voices bounced and echoed around the chimney, making them sound all the more menacing. Dotty suppressed a scream. But she had to wait. Just for a moment longer, just for one minute... And then she saw it: the bricks at the top of the chimney breast, where the wall joined the ceiling, began to creak and crush. The sweeps were entering the playroom.

Quickly Dotty took hold of the chrysalis in the palm of her left hand. It glowed steadily, clear and brittle like blown glass. The chimney breast bulged. Porguss and Poachling were almost upon her. "Magick be gone," Dotty whispered, her mouth close to the charm, closing her hand around it, crushing the chrysalis into a thousand glowing fragments. A boot became visible at the top of the open hearth. They were about to land.

Dotty blew the fragments of the chrysalis towards the open fireplace. As each fragment touched the fire it stuck to it, piercing it, destroying the magical fire surround, returning the cast iron range, piece by piece like a jigsaw in reverse. Porguss and Poachling landed: or, rather, they tried to, but the reinstated range was now in their way. The couple screamed as hands, feet, fingers and toes were forced and crushed into every part of the range.

Porguss shrieked. The cast iron strained and shuddered as it struggled to contain their bulging forms. A foot exploded out of the flue, its owner quite wedged. Poachling roared his outrage as the pair squeezed to a halt in a cloud of soot and brick dust. A single button pinged across the room, torn from Poachling's waistcoat as he ground to an uncomfortable stop. Dotty waited for a few seconds whilst the range finished its straining and swelling as it engulfed the treacherous sweeps entirely. Porguss was still shouting and wailing from deep inside it, like some poor beast trapped in the cavernous belly of a cast iron monster. A muffled outpouring rang from inside the oven.

Walking across to it, Dotty leant down and opened the range door. It was Poachling, his great fat head filling the whole of the oven.

"We'll get you for this!" he bellowed.

"If you can get out, that is," Dotty dared him, confident; triumphant. And with that, she turned on her heel and walked out of Mam's Playroom, all the while Porguss screeching and Poachling roaring after her, shouting with the full force of his rage "We'll get you. WE'LL GET YOU!"

Dotty smiled and closed the playroom door behind her.

*

Well that's the two main problems out of the way Dotty told herself. *Now all I have to do is find a way into Great Uncle Winchester's study.*

Dotty knew that the study door was locked: locked by Strake as it always was in her Great Uncle's absence. She had hoped that Pip might have some skills in the art of lock-breaking, but sadly he did not. He had even become quite offended when Dotty suggested that this might be the case. "What do you think I am?" he exclaimed. "I come from a highly reputable profession, I'll have you know. It's more than my job's worth to do anything that might risk

Chapter 14

breaking the bond of trust we have built up with you ordinary folk."

Pip had dug his hands into his pockets and pouted in such a fashion that Dotty had no option but to apologise profusely to the little sweep. Eventually, after some time and no small amount of grovelling on Dotty's part, Pip forgave her, however. "I'm not the Artful Dodger, you know," he had argued, reproachfully.

The preservation of Pip's reputation was all well and good but from a practical viewpoint of no help to Dotty whatever. The simple fact of the matter was that, for their plan to return the locket to work, Dotty needed to get through a locked door...unless she entered the study via another route entirely, of course.

Putting the next part of her plan into action Dotty raced down the corridor and back to her bedroom. The locket bounced reassuringly against her skin as she ran: safe; sturdy. Pip and Dotty's scheme was working: they were almost there. Still feeling a bit giddy from her maiden chimney-hopping voyage, Dotty stopped for a moment and took a deep breath before stepping once more into an open fireplace. It was difficult to believe that all this was happening to her. Her old life back in Cardiff seemed all at once a distant memory, so far removed from it had she become since her move to Yorkshire only a fortnight earlier.

She checked the locket one last time, fearful that it might have become damaged in her recent flight. But it was just as it had always been, unmarked: untroubled by the dramas that had beset its most recent wearer. Dotty studied the photograph of the dirty boy once more. She wondered who he could be. She supposed she would never find out now. With a small sigh, and steeling herself with one last burst of resolve, Dotty stepped into the chimney.

Whoosh! Whizz! A hop, skip and a jump and Dotty was there already, tumbling; falling, hurtling at great speed towards Great Uncle Winchester's study fireplace. Perhaps she was simply getting used to the sensation, but Dotty had to admit that chimney hopping was altogether a more pleasant experience when not in fear of an imminent squashing, and when not beset with jackdaws on all sides, for that matter.

Dotty skidded to a halt in the open fireplace. Brushing the soot from her clothes she had a sudden sense of naughtiness, standing inside her great uncle's locked study, uninvited and alone. She couldn't help but let out a small giggle. Dotty looked towards the study window. The blind still covered it, what seemed like lamplight seeping through at the edges. Quickly she crossed the room, pulling up the blind to see what lay beyond. The view did not disappoint, for rather than the cold, dark inner courtyard of the Calendar House that one would have expected to see, silent and empty, instead she saw the most wondrous sight, lit with lamplight from numerous gas lamps that illuminated the busy market square beyond.

The cobbled street was the very picture of Christmas, with market stalls selling all manner of gifts: woollen scarves and mittens, winter snow globes, boxes of candies and intricate wooden carvings of all shapes and sizes. There were street sellers selling jacket potatoes and a boy selling roast chestnuts from a great tin drum; mince pies and mulled wine and gingerbread and all manner of sweet treats. Great Uncle Winchester must find this a heaven of his own making, Dotty surmised. And beyond all the stalls, stands and tents there were folk of all shapes and sizes going about their business all glowing, she imagined, with the abundant Christmas cheer that seemed to flood every corner of the square.

Dotty watched through the window as the Christmas scene unfolded before her eyes, laughing in delight as she spotted a sweep, unmistakable because of the tools of his trade, brushes slung across his back as he picked his way through the crowd. And once she had seen one of Pip's kind, barefoot and merry, she couldn't help but see one after another, sweep after sweep, mingling in the lamplight with the market traders. But where was Pip? She couldn't see him anywhere. Perhaps he had been delayed. Dotty noticed that it had begun to snow.

Not to be put off, Dotty set about opening the window, pulling at the window catches, heaving at the sash in an effort to open it. At least she would be ready to hand over the locket to Pip when he arrived, she reasoned. Finally Dotty managed to release the window, lifting the heavy window pane in one enormous effort, the wooden frame squeaking and groaning at the task.

A flurry of snow whipped into the room, the cold wind fresh on her face and arms. She thrust her head out of the window, into the snow and the street that it covered. She strained her eyes, searching for Pip in the lamp light. All at once she heard someone calling her name "Dorothea!" it resonated in greeting.

Dotty was confused. She leant further out of the window, peering through the crowds. "Pip!" she cried. "Pip, is that you?" But then she realised. The voice had not come from the window outside; it had come from inside the house: from the study behind her! So intent was she upon her task that Dotty hadn't noticed the heavy oak study door opening, squeaking on its hinges as it gave with some force. Dotty froze, head still out of the open window. Surely it couldn't be Strake. He simply couldn't have got back from Wales so quickly. But he was the only one with a key to the study! Except for…

Chapter 14

"Now then, young lady," the voice boomed again from behind her. "Is that really the best greeting you can muster for your Great Uncle Winchester?"

Up the Chimney, Down the Chimney

Chapter 15

Home

In which Great Uncle Winchester returns and Dotty has some guests

Great Uncle Winchester stood in the doorway, hair customarily askew, a half-eaten bowl of trifle tucked under one arm, briefcase under the other. Dotty was so pleased to see him that she momentarily forgot the open window and her thoroughly sooty appearance. She ran headlong towards her great uncle, arms outstretched, and hugged and hugged and hugged him as hard as she could, he unable for the moment to reciprocate because his arms were otherwise engaged.

"Dorothea, my dear girl how excellent to see you!" Great Uncle Winchester greeted Dotty with his usual vigour. "I'm so very sorry to not to have been here for you this last week. I say, would you care to join me in a mince pie? They're warm straight from the kitchen." Great Uncle Winchester beamed good-naturedly, producing from under his overcoat a tray of newly-iced mincemeat tarts, still steaming. "I relieved Mrs Gobbins of these on my way through, he winked at Dotty conspiratorially. He still clutched the half-eaten trifle tightly. This was obviously not for sharing.

"Oh, Great Uncle Winchester," Dotty gushed. "I'm sorry, I know I shouldn't be in your study it's just that…oh, I'm so very glad you're home! I've been in so much trouble while you've been gone." She hugged her great uncle again, tears of relief springing to her eyes.

Great Uncle Winchester shuffled awkwardly toward the desk; desserts under each arm, his great niece still attached to his middle. He carefully placed his precious cargo of confectionary down on a rare space between his papers that lay scattered across the desk top.

"On the contrary, dear girl," he remarked, "I understand you've been doing rather admirably in my absence." Dotty took a step back, a little shocked. "Ah, and here's Pip now." Great Uncle Winchester looked over to the window, waving a greeting at Dotty's friend.

Chapter 15

Dotty gawped at the pair in disbelief. She was convinced Pip had never mentioned knowing her great uncle before. But surely that meant he knew about…

"Come in, dear boy, come in," he gestured. "And close that window will you? It's blowing a gale in here." Pip hopped over the window ledge and did as he was told, pulling the sash shut with a thud.

"Evening, Mr Winchester, Sir," replied Pip civilly, doffing his cap in respect. "Good to see you home, Sir."

Great Uncle Winchester gave Pip a fond pat on the back. "Do help yourself to a mince pie, won't you? There's a good lad." Pip didn't need to be asked twice and tucked in with alacrity.

Dotty stood agape as the two exchanged pleasantries. She was dumfounded; gobsmacked: in every sense a codfish. Great Uncle Winchester seemed not to notice Dotty standing stationary like a giant rabbit caught in the headlights and prattled on to Pip as if nothing out of the ordinary was transpiring here at all.

Perhaps he is very tired from his journey, Dotty thought. *He is an old man after all. Yes, that must be it*, she concluded. *Clearly he hasn't noticed that I'm standing in a locked room covered from head to foot in coal dust; that a small dirty and barefooted boy has just climbed through his open window and that there appears to be an entire other-worldly civilisation carrying on its daily business right outside his study window.*

"So glad you two managed to get together whilst I was away," he continued. "I had so wanted to introduce you before I had to leave so suddenly, but you know how it is, business…"

Pip? It was Pip to whom Great Uncle Winchester had wanted to introduce Dotty? And all the while she had assumed Geoff was the friend her great uncle had been so keen for her to meet.

Dotty took the opportunity to glare at Pip, accusations flying from her eyes *"You know him?"* she glared at him, without speaking. *"You know my Great Uncle Winchester and you didn't bother to mention this?!"*

Pip shuffled a bit, cheeks still full of mince pie, wincing a *"sorry,"* in voiceless reply.

"Now you must excuse me for a moment, my dears," Great Uncle Winchester continued to speak in between mouthfuls of mince pie, his speech slurred and broken by a mass of mincemeat and pastry. "It's been a long journey back from London and I simply have to make myself more comfortable. Bunions, you know."

Great Uncle Winchester disappeared under the great oak writing desk for a moment, scouting around between the piles of papers in order to produce an enormous pair of novelty carpet slippers, in the shape of dog's heads. Finishing his latest mouthful of pastry, he proceeded to don the dog slippers, casting aside his heavy weather-beaten brogues.

Chapter 15

Still mute, Dotty's eyes strayed back to the window. Despite being shut it was surprisingly noisy outside: a busy street, not at all in keeping with the quietude of the study.

"Which reminds me," queried her great uncle, "where *is* Geoff? I trust he has been behaving himself?" Great Uncle Winchester poked his head under the desk once again, searching for his furry companion in his usual hiding place.

Whilst her great uncle's gaze was averted, Pip took the opportunity to renew his silent conversation with Dotty, gesticulating wildly at her to regain her attention. *"Where is it?"* he mouthed, swallowing a last mouthful of pie. *"Where is the locket?"*

In all the excitement Dotty had almost forgotten the reason for her presence in her great uncle's study. They had to return the Calendar House Key to the Sweeps' Council!

"It's here!" Dotty mouthed. *"I have it around my neck!"* Dotty held the locket aloft, pointing to it with her free hand theatrically.

Just as she did so Great Uncle Winchester righted himself, interrupting their silent conversation with his own silent curse as he banged his head on the underside of the great wooden desk.

"Aha! And I see you have your mother's locket," he exclaimed, rubbing his injured crown. "It's so good to see it again. We thought it was lost for such a long time." Great Uncle Winchester smiled fondly at it, as if greeting an old friend. "May I?" He held out his hand to touch it.

Speechless, Dotty stood impassive, letting her great uncle handle the locket. Turning it over in his hand he smiled reminiscently at the picture in the back of the case. "Ah yes," he smiled. "Your grandfather was a handsome youth, back in the day, Dorothea." Dotty opened her mouth to speak but only managed a small squeak in acknowledgement.

Seeing she was in need of saving, Pip interjected:

"We need to get the Key back to the Council, Sir; and quickly. The rogue sweeps, Sir, they know we have it."

"No, my dear boy, I don't think that will be necessary." Great Uncle Winchester gave his shock reply.

"But, Sir, the Council, Sir!" Pip contested. Dotty watched their exchange, confounded.

Great Uncle Winchester was firm now, his face rarely serious. "Master Peregrine, the locket has always remained within the Winchester family and I see no reason to change that now," he stated. Dotty stood: her heart in her mouth. Could he really do this? Her great uncle continued, "Dorothea is a direct descendant of the maker of this chimney key and in my opinion she has shown herself a more than responsible custodian of it. It is clear to me that she should continue as its guardian."

"And I daresay you could make good use of it, couldn't you, my dear?" Dotty's great uncle turned to her with a questioning smile. "Chimney travel is so much more convenient than Skype, don't you find?" Dotty was flabbergasted.

"But the Council, Sir!" Pip persisted.

"It's not for you to trouble yourself with the Council, Pip," Great Uncle Winchester soothed. "I will clear it with them in the morning. First thing: I promise you faithfully. Here, have another mince pie." He proffered the tray.

"Now off you go, Pip, and we'll hear no more about it, if you please."

"Very well, Mr Winchester, Sir," replied Pip, turning to Dotty. "I expect I will be seeing you very soon, Miss, if I'm not mistaken." And with that he hopped back over the window ledge and into the courtyard, and in an instant was lost in the crowd.

With Pip gone, Great Uncle Winchester turned his attentions once more to Dotty. "My dear girl, if you don't mind it's been a long day and I have a spaniel to unearth. Could we finish our catch up tomorrow morning? We have rather a lot of catching up to do, wouldn't you say?" Dotty nodded in agreement, still struggling to find words to adequately match the situation in which she found herself.

"Right you are then. Let's meet bright and early. Shall we say, nine o'clock?" he smiled.

"And, darling child, a bath before bedtime might be an idea, don't you think? You're a mite dusty."

Just at that moment a rather flustered and habitually floured Gobby appeared at the study door. "The mince pies' she complained. 'I'm missing a tray. Have you seen…?"

"Mrs Gobbins, how charming it is to see you." Great Uncle Winchester broke her off. "Yes they were quite delicious: I really must congratulate you on yet another successful creation." Great Uncle Winchester handed Gobby a now empty tray.

"I say, Mrs Gobbins," he went on before the disgruntled cook could protest further. "Won't you be a dear and light some fires around the house for us? I feel a bit of a chill and we don't want any uninvited…*drafts*….getting in, now do we?" he looked knowingly at Dotty, a twinkle in his eye. "Now where *is* that dog?"

"Geoff will be hiding in the boot room, I suspect, Great Uncle Winchester," Dotty grinned. Great Uncle Winchester was quite simply ace.

"Thank you, my dear. Now off you run," he shooed her. "Oh, and, Dorothea, before you go, I wonder if I might ask you: would you mind terribly calling me Winnie? I have to confess dear girl I've always struggled with titles and I've never really liked the name Winchester: too formal, do you see?"

Dotty beamed. "No problem, Winnie," she said.

"Thank you, dear girl, much obliged." And with the faintest glimmer of a wink he shuffled off out of the study.

*

Back upstairs Dotty languished lazily in the sumptuous bubble-filled tub, soaking away the dust and all the trouble and excitement of a very busy and unusual day. A fire blazed in the bathroom fireplace; Gobby stoked and prodded at it, chatting away at Dotty in her usual verbose manner as she did so.

"Now come along, young lady, out you get. I have so much to do before tomorrow you know. The house needs to be spick and span for our guests arriving in the morning, and there are all the Christmas decorations to put up too."

"Guests? What guests?" asked Dotty. She wasn't aware that they were expecting visitors to the house.

"Why didn't Mr Winchester tell you?" started Gobby in surprise. "Your friend Sylvia and her father are coming to spend Christmas with us, at Mr Winchester's invitation. He thought you would enjoy the company."

Jubilant, Dotty sprang into action, leaping out of the bath and grabbing for a towel. Really, this day couldn't get any better. Well, almost.

"It's going to be a late night," Gobby continued, without taking breath. Dotty scrubbed at her hair with the towel. "I have to clean out all the fire grates before I can light them again. There's soot everywhere," Gobby groused. "All over the good carpets, on the drapes, honestly you wouldn't give them credit."

"*Them*, Mrs Gobbins?" Dotty asked, pulling on her pyjamas.

"Why the jackdaws, dear," Gobby replied, ushering Dotty into her bedroom, pulling back the bedcovers and gesturing for Dotty to hop in. "That's always been the problem with this house," she grumbled. "Just far too many jackdaws in the chimneys."

Gobby pulled the covers up under Dotty's chin. "Well, good night my dear, and sleep well." And with that she kissed Dotty fondly on the forehead and melted quietly out of the room.

DOTTY

and the Chimney Thief

Emma Warner-Reed

Chapter 1

Missing!

*In which Sylv tells Dotty about Joe Raman's
disappearance and Gobby scolds the dog*

The familiar image of Dotty's best friend looked
out at her from the iPad. Her bottom lip
trembled, her complexion ashen. Dotty didn't
ever think she'd seen Sylv looking so upset.

"Oh my word Sylv, what's happened?"
Dotty asked. "Are you okay?"

"Can you come now, Dot? Can you just
come to Cardiff? Please! I need your help."

Dotty looked exasperated. "Is it your
homework again? Look, you know I can't come
hopping down the chimney every time you call.
It's just not practical."

Missing!

"It's not homework, Dot. It's Joe. He's...well, he's *vanished*!" Sylv's bottom lip quivered more violently and she broke into a sob.

"Vanished? What do you mean, 'vanished'? Are you sure?"

"Yes I'm sure." Sylv looked cross. "He's gone missing. Plain disappeared. Look, Dot, I really need you to come. *Right now*."

"Okay, Sylv. I'm coming. What have the police said?"

"That's the thing," wailed Sylv. "The police don't seem to know anything. They can't explain what happened. Joe went missing from his bedroom but he sleeps on the top floor and you can only get to his room by going through his sister, Jazz's. There are a couple of skylights in the roof, but they're way too small even for Joe to climb through, and you know how small he is.

Jazz swears that she was in her bedroom all night and that she never saw him. But without walking past her there's just no other way he could have got out."

Dotty waited as her friend paused for a moment, convulsing with sobs, trying to catch her breath.

"The police are saying either he must have run away or, worse, that his family's disappeared him! But of course that's not true. It can't be. Oh Dot, it's terrible. Joe's dad's awful upset."

Dotty tried to think of what her Mam used to say to her when she was crying. "Okay Sylv, now take some deep breaths," Dotty soothed, using the most reassuring grown-up voice she could muster. "It's awful about Joe, of course it is. But if the police can't work it out, what do you think *I* can do?"

"Isn't it obvious?" Sylv replied, her tense, pale face staring up from the screen. "The police don't know all the facts, do they? I mean, if he didn't go out through the door, he must have left another way – like up the chimney."

Dotty inhaled sharply, shocked. It hadn't occurred to her that a sweep might be involved. A rogue sweep, even. This was the worst kind of news. Her mind raced with possibilities.

"Oh Dot, you've just got to come," Sylv moaned. "I need you here now. You're my best friend. Come on *butt*[1], I know you can help. Puhleeeaase! I want you here with me so we can figure this out together."

In truth, Dotty had been on board since she heard the word 'chimney'. "All right, Sylv, I'm said I'm coming, didn't I? But just hang on until after dinner, can you? Gobby'll go nuts if I miss my tea. You know what she's like."

"Yeah, okay," Slyv conceded with a sniff.

"Right, then," Dotty instructed. "Just sit tight. I'm on my way."

*

---

[1] Welsh for "friend".

The supper bell trilled impatiently in the distance. It was the cook, Mrs Gobbins (affectionately named 'Gobby' by the girls), calling her for supper.

Dotty's life had changed so much over the last few months that it seemed almost impossible now to remember the way things had been before. She still felt like the same feisty little Welsh girl inside, but since the tragic loss of her parents last November, everything was different. Her old life back in Cardiff seemed a world and a half away.

The accident had made the news.

"Local Couple Die with Family Pets in House Fire. Daughter Narrowly Escapes Blaze"

Dotty was haunted by memories of that night. If only she hadn't nagged Mam and Dad to have a firework party in the back garden of their small, suburban home. She remembered how excited she and Sylv had been, running home from school that afternoon, giggling and laughing.

And she remembered with bittersweet regret how much effort her dad had put into the display, buying up every firework from Eddie Raman's Corner shop, as Eddie's son, Joe, had taken great delight in telling the girls when they stopped in for sweets on their way home from school.

But now she needed to get to Cardiff and to
Sylv. She had to help Joe, if she could. The cross-
sounding bell continued to ting-a-ling in the
background, calling her impatiently. Dotty tutted
to herself. Could she get away with it if she left
right now? No, probably not. Gobby would be
doing her numbers if Dotty let her supper go
cold.

Dotty gestured to a fat old brown-and-white
spaniel that lay across the doorway, forming quite
an effective draught excluder.

"Come on, Geoff. Dinner time!"

Geoff jumped up eagerly, the years visibly
dropping off him at the mention of food.
Together the two hurtled down the back stairs
that led into the kitchen.

"Sorry, Mrs Gobbins," Dotty apologised as
she poked her head around the kitchen door,
anticipating the roasting she was about to receive
for being slow to answer the bell. She tried to
look casual whilst attempting to hide Geoff's
rather large outline behind her legs, only too
aware of the cook's dislike of dogs in her precious
kitchen.

The old cook was ladling homemade
strawberry jam out of a vat of the stuff that
teetered precariously on the corner of the dresser,
slopping it into a smaller glass serving dish. As
usual, she looked as if she had entered into a
battle with the flour bin and lost.

Missing!

The ladle slipped out of the cook's hands and landed back in the vat with a juicy *thwack*, splattering her with small sticky globules of jam. Together with the dusting of flour, it made her look like she had a severe case of strawberry jam measles. Dotty supressed a giggle.

"And about time, too," Gobby snapped as she man-handled the glass lid back on to the oversized container. "I thought you were never coming! Well, tuck in, girl. There are ham sandwiches and toasted teacakes, and there's a nice slab of Christmas cake there. Oh," she stopped herself. "I forgot the cheese."

She bustled off in the direction of the larder, still covered in flour and spotted with jam.

"There's a nice piece of Wensleydale out back. I'll go fetch it."

"There's really no need, Mrs Gobbins, I..." she trailed off. Gobby was gone. Dotty had never understood the Yorkshire custom of eating fruit cake with a slice of cheese, or indeed of eating Christmas cake in March. Both seemed plain weird to her. But there was no point trying to change the woman's mind once she had it set on something, so she just let the old cook put it on the table with the other tea things.

Dotty scooped up a plate, hurriedly filling it with food from the table that she did like. She needed to get to Sylv's. She grabbed a couple of ham sandwiches for starters, the freshly-baked gammon spilling out of the soft homemade bread, butter dripping from them where the warmth of the meat had melted it. Her mouth watered. Despite her haste to leave, she was actually quite hungry. She spooned a couple of round, crunchy pickled onions out of a jar and onto her plate. "Want one, Geoff?" she teased the overweight spaniel.

Geoff grimaced visibly, and Dotty laughed as he sniffed rather more hopefully at the baked ham. She knew that Geoff hated pickled onions, although from experience she also knew that he wasn't past giving one a good suck if nothing better was on offer.

She was about to make a swift exit when Gobby came whirling back into the room with a gigantic round of cheese in hand. The ample woman fought to find a place for it on the already-full farmhouse table. "There," she said, giving a satisfied nod. "That should be enough for a modest supper."

Dotty snorted, her mouth full of sandwich. Modest! This table had never seen modest.

"I'd better get Mr Winchester's tea tray ready. He'll be eating in his study tonight."

Dotty had never known Great Uncle Winchester to eat a meal anywhere *except* in his study. She raised an eyebrow in acknowledgement.

Gobby busied herself piling a tray high with sandwiches and teacakes, and fresh slices of Battenburg cake (one of the cook's specialities and Winchester's particular favourite). Then she set about warming the teapot on the great cast iron range, unearthing a tin of her employer's best gunpowder tea.

Dotty crammed her mouth full of sandwich, half sitting, half standing, as she tried to find an excuse to leave the table. Meanwhile Geoff skulked under the great scrubbed kitchen table top. Dotty suspected that he was waiting for the perfect moment to snaffle something from around the heavily laden table's edges. Although when Gobby took the tea tray out to his master, the dog would have plenty of opportunity to steal a meaty snack, she thought.

"Well, that should do." Gobby gave a satisfied nod, surveying the heavily-laden tea tray.

"Why don't I take that," asked Dotty, seeing her chance to escape.

"No, dear. You eat your supper. I'll call Mr Strake. Sit yourself back down dear."

Dotty had no choice but to oblige her. Gobby stepped neatly over to a small square panel on the kitchen wall and pressed one of the buttons. A bell rang in the distance. A moment passed and there was a cursory knock on the kitchen door. Not waiting for an answer, the door opened.

"You rang, Mrs Gobbins?" A tall, lanky figure stooped in the doorway. It was Strake. Dotty gave an involuntary shudder. Even if Gobby had not summoned him, instinct would have told Dotty it was her great uncle's personal secretary before she ever saw him. The man appeared to carry about with him an uncomfortable air. It wasn't anything Dotty could see, of course. Just a bad feeling that seemed to follow him, infecting everything Strake came into contact with. If it had been visible, Dotty imagined Strake would have been stalking around bearing a damp, dark brown fog of sorts on that unnaturally curved back of his.

Strake, likewise, seemed to resent Dotty's presence in the kitchen. He twitched, nervously. No discussion had ever taken place between them about his thwarted attempt to steal the Calendar House Key from Dotty and her friends; or of how his failure had been received by the villains that he had tried to steal it for: the awful rogue sweep traders, Porguss and Poachling. Dotty reckoned they must have given him a roasting! Whatever had happened, Strake seemed to fear her now and, Dotty had to admit, she wasn't displeased with the result.

Even months after the event, Dotty was still angry at the thought of what these three had tried to do – stealing the precious Calendar House Key, so long thought lost. And all so that they could use the ancient sweeps' magick to take innocent children from their beds, forcing them up the chimneys and away into a life of slavery in the cold and the dark of the world of the sweeps. She glowered at Strake. He winced in reply.

Missing!

You could have cut the atmosphere with a knife, although, as usual, Gobby seemed blissfully unaware of anything other than the nose in front of her face.

"Mr Strake, would you take Mr Winchester's tea tray in to him? I'm waiting on a batch of Welsh cakes and I don't want them to burn."

Strake quickly resumed his usual superlative air. "Certainly, Mrs Gobbins: nothing is too much trouble for Mr Winchester, of course." He eyed the cook, rather pointedly, Dotty thought, as her were suggesting that the cook's priorities should lay with their employer, rather than with her baking.

"Well, that's settled, then," she trilled. "You'd better hurry, Mr Strake, the tea will be getting cold. I've warmed the pot, but—"

Strake interrupted Gobby's speech by whisking the tray out of her hands with long, spidery fingers and, without another word, beating a hasty retreat out of the kitchen. He backed out of the doorway, as was customary for him. Dotty knew that he did this as a show of politeness or respect, but she couldn't help but think that Strake's real reason for not showing his back to the occupant of the room he was leaving, was for fear that they might be unable to resist the urge to stick a knife in it.

No sooner had the air cleared of the unpleasant atmosphere caused by Strake's presence in the room, but another figure loomed at the rear kitchen door. It was Kenny, the gardener. Kenny cut an altogether different figure, leaning heavily on the door frame in his usual casual manner. He smelled of dirt and earth and old tobacco. Dotty liked Kenny. She beamed at his arrival.

"Hiya, Kenny," she mumbled through a mouthful of teacake.

"Hello, Miss Dotty," replied Kenny. His face remained serious but a twinkle in his eye gave away the old Yorkshireman's affection for her. "Mrs Gobbins, have you seen, Geoff? I have orders for his bath."

Geoff flattened himself against the stone flag floor. Dotty watched the spaniel's vain attempt to make himself undetectable with amusement. Clearly he understood the word 'bath'.

"Certainly not, Kenneth. You know I don't allow dogs in my kitchen," Gobby snorted. She really didn't like dogs, and in particular Geoff, Dotty guessed on account of the fact that he was always stealing food out of the larder, or even off the kitchen table if he could get away with it.

Dotty shuffled impatiently, itching to get going. She really wanted to see Sylv now. She studied the floor, trying not to give away the spaniel's hiding place under the table, but it didn't help. Kenny's sharp old eyes quickly spotted Geoff's brown and white paws poking out from beneath the tablecloth.

"Mrs Gobbins, I think you'll find you have a stowaway," he remarked wryly.

"Oh my legs and arms! That dog will be the death of me!" Gobby threw her flour covered hands dramatically into the air.

With two short strides, Kenny had the unfortunate mutt by the collar and was dragging him ungraciously out of his hiding place and the warmth of the kitchen, to his soapy fate at the mercy of the garden hose.

The cook turned to Dotty. "I assume you knew about this," she accused.

At last, Dotty had found the perfect moment to make herself scarce. Hastily, she made her excuses. "Right, Mrs Gobbins, I'm off to, er, *Skype* Sylv".

And before the irate housekeeper could scold her any further, Dotty got down from the table and bid a hasty retreat back to her bedroom.

Once there, Dotty took a deep breath, holding the locket firmly in the palm of her hand, as was her habit. Her fingers enveloped the heavy gold lozenge, its sturdy chain still safely around her neck.

It wasn't that Dotty wasn't used to chimney travel by now. Dotty had travelled this way many times since the events leading up to last Christmas and her discovery of the Calendar House Key: a magical locket that her dear

Chapter 1

departed mother had buried deep inside the playroom chimney so many years before.

She thought back to the first time she had seen anyone travel through the chimneys: the shock appearance of Pip, the apprentisweep, flying down her own bedroom chimney and appearing, soot-covered, on her hearth. And her discovery of a secret world of magical chimney sweeps that seemed to reside deep within the walls of the Calendar House itself. Back then she could never have known that her mother's hidden locket would turn out to be not just a piece of jewellery, but a key: a magical key that allowed ordinary folk to use the ancient sweeps' magick to travel from one chimney to another, reaching almost anywhere in an instant, as long as it had a hearth.

This locket was one of the few remaining portals created by the sweeps in times gone by, when magical and ordinary folk mingled together freely and openly, the sweeps keeping and guarding the hearths of all men and women here in Dotty's ordinary world.

And so it was that Dotty was well used to zipping up and down the chimneys; to visit Sylv in Cardiff, mostly (it beat TransRail), but also sometimes to travel from room to room within the vast mansion house that since the tragic death of her parents had become her home. My, what a strange and magical home it had turned out to be, Dotty thought.

Nevertheless, chimney travel was still an odd feeling. She closed her eyes for a moment. It wasn't exactly claustrophobic; it was over too quickly to have time to think about being crammed and whizzed through the thousands of tiny tunnels and passages that made up the network of chimneys both within the Calendar House and beyond. But it was most certainly a strange sensation. It made Dotty's stomach flip, just like one of those swing boat rides at the fairground. Still, she had no time to muse over that now. She took one more deep breath.

"Hold on, Sylv, I'm on my way." Dotty said to herself. And then, without further ado, she stepped straight into the fire.

ABOUT THE AUTHOR

Emma Warner-Reed is a qualified lawyer, academic, legal journalist and author. Emma also has her own children's book review channel on YouTube: DOTTY about BOOKS, which recommends the best reads in picture books, early/young independent readers and children's chapter books.

Emma lives in a rural setting on the edge of the Yorkshire Dales with her husband, four small children and a plethora of animals, some of whom are more domesticated than others!

To date the first book in the series, DOTTY and the Calendar House Key, released in 2015, has received significant acclaim including the Literary Classics Silver Award for children's fantasy fiction, an exclusively five star rating on Amazon, the official Seal of Approval from Literary Classics and Honourable Mentions at the Los Angeles, New York, Amsterdam and Paris Book Festival Awards. DOTTY and the Chimney Thief is the second novel in The DOTTY Series. Look out for Dotty's third adventure, DOTTY and the Dream Catchers, coming soon!

Please feel free to contact Emma for interviews, quotes or comments about her writing via any of the methods listed on the contact page on the website. For regular news, reviews and updates on The DOTTY Series, subscribe to the DOTTY mailing list at www.thedottyseries.com, or follow Emma on Twitter or Facebook.

What people have to say about DOTTY:

"Author Emma Warner-Reed has penned a magnificent children's book with suspense that builds as young readers are drawn into the mystery surrounding Dotty's new home. Dotty and the Calendar House Key is highly recommended for home and school libraries and has earned the Literary Classics Seal of Approval."

Literary Classics Book Reviews
Amazon

"Dotty and the Calendar House Key has truly fired my daughter's imagination for the first time since Harry Potter. Beautifully written and exciting. The Secret Garden meets Diagon Alley. Fabulous!"

Alexandra Vere
Harrogate

"My son has just read the first [book] and thinks it's brilliant - high praise since he has very decided opinions about what he reads."

P. Uglow
Harrogate

"I really liked the [first] book. It was a bit scary when Dotty found herself in Uncle Winchester's private study. But most of the books I read are a bit scary so that was okay. I would read the other books in the series. Go Team Dotty!"

Betty, age 7
Amazon

"*Enchanting, innocent and lovely with just the right amount of modern technology...a great read for a grown up 7 year old! She loved it... When is the next one coming out?*"

A. Little
Amazon

"*I read [DOTTY and the Chimney Thief] to the children tonight and they were instantly back to being as gripped as they were by the first book. They both laughed out loud at the wonderful descriptions of Gobby in the kitchen covered in flour (again) and the way she asked Kenny to remove Geoff! They cannot wait to find out what happens next.*"

J. Johnson
Stallingborough

For further information and updates on The DOTTY Series visit:
www.thedottyseries.com

22974305R00130

Printed in Great Britain
by Amazon